DEAD GIRL DIARIES

Marianne Paul

BookLand press

TORONTO, CANADA

Copyright © 2009 by Marianne Paul

This book is a work of fiction. Names, characters, places and incidents are either the product of the author's imagination or are used fictitiously, and any resemblance to actual persons living or dead, events or locales is entirely coincidental. All trademarks are properties of their respective owners.

All rights reserved. No part of this publication may be reproduced or transmitted in any form or by any means, electronic or mechanical, including photocopying, recording, or any information storage and retrieval system, without the written permission of the publisher.

Bookland Press Inc.
6021 Yonge Street
Suite 1010
Toronto, Ontario M2M 3W2
www.booklandpress.com

Editor: Robert Morgan

Printed and bound in Canada.

Library and Archives Canada Cataloguing in Publication

Paul, Marianne
    Dead girl diaries / Marianne Paul.

ISBN 978-0-9783793-8-4

    I. Title.

PS8581.A829D43 2008   C813'.54   C2009-906204-3

*For Art,
who believes in the otherworld,
and shares the family history*

CHAPTER 1

Maxine thought that she didn't know her grandfather since she had no conscious memory of him. That's because Amos died when she was three years old. He was found ice-cold and dead of a heart attack in the garden, wrapped around the pea plants, falling in such a way to avoid crushing them. Maxine visited her grandfather once, spending three days on the train with Golda to reach the prairie farm, staying for a month, then returning home to Ontario, never again to see Amos. Because she was a toddler at the time of her first and only visit, she didn't remember walking with the old man along the neat garden rows, her shoes squishing in the soil. She didn't remember leading the way, too young to walk steadily by herself, Amos following closely behind, bent over and holding her pudgy little hands in his own. Maxine so tiny that she easily walked under his legs, his legs like the arch of a high tower, his head the steeple. His thick white hair so like the clouds that hung above her in the sky that she did not differentiate between the two. Neither did she remember the flowers that Amos picked and pushed into her face, wrapping her in sweet perfume. Sniff, he'd say, and Maxine would sniff deeply. Nor Amos picking a peapod from the stem, making a snapping sound as he opened the pod between his fingers, Maxine wobbling on her feet, looking up at her grandfather. Amos bending over, bringing the clouds to her, his old knees cracking, the little girl reaching up, feeling the clouds between her fingertips. Amos putting a pea into her mouth, fingers thick and rough against her young skin, cupping her face clumsily, tenderly, as if she were precious and might break like fine china.

Amos died in the very same garden on the day Maxine's little sister, Movida, was born. According to family legend, this is what happened. The first part is true and readily corroborated: Golda didn't give birth easily. She didn't spit out her children like peas through a peashooter, one enormous exhalation and out they flew, lustily hollering, wildly kicking, ready to take root and make their mark on the world. Each birth was like pushing a square peg out of a round hole, and Movida was no exception. She chose to go down the tube-slide feet first, wrapping the umbilical cord under one arm, over a shoulder, and around her tiny neck.

The second part of the family legend may or may not be true, and cannot be corroborated. This part says that Amos willingly laid himself down in that garden, sinking to his knees to avoid crushing the pea plants at the very same moment in time that baby Movida struggled to extricate herself from the cord, Golda screeching in pain and huffing and panting to no avail. Amos must have had a premonition, Golda said later, a statement that quickly became entrenched as family truth. He must have made a pact with the angel of death, traded his life for his granddaughter's. How else could you explain it, the cord suddenly loosening, the pain suddenly leaving, Movida slipping out of her mother and into the world with sweet ease?

Maxine wrote a third part to the family legend. She kept the literary addition to herself, rolled it out from the safekeeping of her memory every once in a while. It went like this: On the day of her grandfather's death, dancing apparitions visited him in the garden, reached down amongst the pea plants, lifted him weightlessly to his feet. At first Amos was groggy, and then light of spirit, light of feet. He danced happily down the road with the row of ghost-girls and jigged off into oblivion.

✧ ✧ ✧

Now that I am Maxine's ghost, for lack of a better word, I wonder if Maxine truly believed in ghosts. Oh, she played Ouija board as a teenager when her mother, Golda, went through that séance stage. If pressed, she might have said she thought there was life after death, but looking back from my current vantage point, I'm not sure Maxine really knew what she believed, if she had had enough time or inclination to commit to such a thing as belief.

Golda, on the other hand, committed wholeheartedly to the existence of supernatural entities such as ghosts and guardian angels. When Maxine was little and afraid of the dark, Golda taught her to say these words: "Get thee behind me Satan, get thee away, I'm a soldier of the Lord's today." The verse was followed by the sign of the cross and saying: "Father, Son and Holy *Ghost*." It worked. Maxine always felt better after she completed the ritual. Felt safe.

Sometimes Golda gathered the family together around the kitchen table to sing hymns. They would clap and sway and warble off-key. "Swing low sweet chariot coming for to carry me home" was one such song lyric. Another: "All night, all day, angels watching over me my Lord."

On occasion, Golda even felt the presence of her guardian angel in the silence of the house, when the children slept or were at school. She put her palm on the Holy Bible and swore to Maxine that she had heard the distant beating of wings and felt a wind brush against her cheek. But that wasn't Golda's only brush with the otherworldly. Sitting in the living room one afternoon, watching a soap opera, she felt a droplet fall on the back of her hand and roll across her skin. The droplet was oily smooth. Not oily from a car, but Bible oily, with a sweet fragrance and soothing touch, like the perfume Mary had used to bathe the feet of Jesus. There was no other explanation for that droplet than the heavenly. No other explanation, but the spirit world sending a message trying to warn Golda about impending doom. To one of her loved ones, she figured, but to which one she couldn't tell. "They're crying for us in heaven," Golda said. "Crying real tears."

For a month following the droplet, Golda watched her children very carefully. Took their temperatures excessively and treated any hints of a fever. Made them look both ways before they crossed the road. Exhorted them to watch out for strangers. Double-checked the locks and window latches each night before she went to bed. Made them kneel at their beds and say extra-long prayers, God bless Mommy, God bless Daddy, God bless Adeline, God bless Peter, God bless Movida, God bless all the little children in the world, and most of all, God bless Maxine.

Golda believed guardian angels and ghosts existed in close proximity to the living, in a dimension gyrating in a slightly shifted orbit, or at a slightly different wave frequency. She called this other world a parallel universe. Golda explained it to Maxine in this way:

"It's just like my washing machine," she said.

"What is?" Maxine asked as Golda pushed the ancient Hoover washing machine from the corner (where it neatly fit when not in use) to the kitchen sink, and hooked the hose to the faucet.

"Parallel universes," Golda answered.

The Hoover washing machine consisted of two side-by-side tubs in the same console, one square tub for washing the clothes, one cylindrical tub to rinse and spin them. It was the spin cycle that caught Golda's fancy. "Come and look," Golda said.

In the middle of the spin cycle, she lifted the lid. The machine whirred madly, threatening to take off like a helicopter. The barrel of the tub spun so fast that the clothes could not be distinguished but whirled by in a blur, pressed flat against the sides by centrifugal force.

"See?"

"I don't see anything."

"My point exactly," Golda said, a touch of annoyance in her voice for having to explain the obvious to her daughter. "The clothes exist. You just can't see them because they are spinning at an extremely fast rate."

The spin cycle neared an end. The gyrating of the tub slowed until the clothes took shape again, blue jeans and a plaid shirt, a work sock, and her father's blue jockey underwear. "And that's us," Golda said, speaking with the confident smugness of Einstein explaining the theory of relativity to a layman. She motioned towards the slowing tub. "The parallel universe is here, right now, all around us. We just can't see it, but that doesn't mean it's not there."

Golda was not the only one in Maxine's family who believed in supernatural beings. Maxine's father, George, did too. George believed in ghosts. Had seen ghosts. Really. Well, maybe not really. George appropriated the ghost story of his father, Amos, Maxine's grandfather. George retold it as if it were his own story, used third person in the telling but with the force and intimacy and ringing endorsement of truth that comes with the first person, as if he were a player in the event itself, at very least an eyewitness. But if push came to shove, George would rather not have seen the ghost himself, content to tell the tale through the eyes of his father. While Golda delighted in the supernatural, George feared it, kept ghosts at arm's length. His thoughts on the topic could be summed up like this:

If you can help it, don't disturb the dead.

You don't want them to take notice of you.

Better to just let them float in and out of your reality as they wish.

In the ghost story that George retold, his father, Amos, saw a row of dancing girls. The apparitions linked hands in a row, danced lightly on their feet, so lightly that they flew, their toes never touching the ground. They danced in a line that stretched across the dirt lane leading from the old farmhouse, four of them, as if they had nary a care in the world. They danced to the accompaniment of accordion music, a lively tune that Amos didn't recognize, never heard before that evening, and never heard again. They danced in the dark along the lonely prairie road, no other beings in sight, ghostly or otherwise, except Amos, no other sound but the accordion, the night itself silent. They danced towards him. Drew closer and closer until they were upon him, passed through him, straight through, never dropping hands, never acknowledging his presence, as if he were of the otherworld and not them. Amos spun around, but the line of dancing girls had evaporated into thin air, taking the accordion music with them, leaving only Amos and the silence of the dark prairie night.

I wonder if Golda and George ever catch a glimpse of Maxine, if some version of their daughter haunts them. Not me, of course, I'm here, in the otherworld. But maybe impressions of Maxine, remnants hanging around them like breath marking the air on a cold brisk evening. Maxine dancing lightly under the canopy of trees that arch over the road by their white stucco house, her ghost feet never touching the earth, dancing right past them and down the street. I wonder if they have seen Maxine in the garden among the rows of zinnias and bachelor buttons and peas, bending gently to sniff the flowers, as if she is a stem bowing to the wind. If they have seen her lingering at the side of the house where remnants of the little graves of insects lie unnoticed, funeral services Maxine conducted when she was a child. If they have seen her catching fireflies in the dead of the night, putting stars into a bottle, the hem of her white gown swirling around her knees like clouds, feathers from the wings of angels.

CHAPTER 2

One day when she was alive and on the way home from her journalism course at Carleton University, Maxine stopped at a corner convenience store and bought an *Ottawa Citizen* and an ice-cream bar. Her homework assignment: to study an obituary, take note of the customary form, and then write one about herself as if she were dead, to look at her life and then condense it into two hundred words or less.

"Afraid there won't be anything to say?" the professor had deadpanned when the class emitted a unified groan. "Ah, immortal youth. Maybe you think you won't die. Everybody dies sooner or later, some sooner than later. Good thing. Who'd buy the newspaper otherwise? Natural disasters, and unnatural disasters, and murders and obituaries, that's what sells newspapers. That's the field of study you've chosen."

Maxine stuffed the *Ottawa Citizen* under her arm, bit into the ice-cream bar and felt the cold hit a nerve like death itself. It was the autumn of Maxine's university career, of her life, too, for that matter, but of course, she didn't know that at this specific moment in time. Maxine hadn't started university by taking journalism, but switched majors. She wanted to experience life, not simply hide behind books, behind words of authors, many who had died long ago and had no understanding of modern times. Don't get me wrong, she added when she talked it over with her boyfriend, Ben. She enjoyed reading books, just didn't want to make their study her life's profession.

"How about becoming a paramedic or an ER nurse?" Ben had asked. "Or join a youth corp, volunteer for an aid position in Africa, work on a kibbutz for a year. You'd experience life in those jobs."

"Too much life," Maxine had said.

She didn't want to be immersed in life, and therefore death, the two inextricably linked in those kinds of jobs. She didn't want blood on her hands, on her clothes, trying to put back together accident victims, or shooting victims, or rape victims, or murder victims. Didn't want to be overwhelmed, day in and day out, night in and night out, by people she couldn't fix, children she couldn't feed, tragedies she couldn't change. Journalism allowed her to find balance, satisfied the strange need for compassion and reticence, action and non-action that so often governed her existence. Let her study life in the third person. Third person was safe. It put space between herself and her subject. Allowed her to come close, to examine, but not be consumed. Allowed her to make statements, but not take centre stage. Allowed her to commit, since she had chosen the topic, the slant of the article, whom to interview, what quotations to include, but not to commit whole-heartedly, not put herself on the frontline with the first person. Dispassionate compassion is what journalism allowed Maxine.

That evening, Maxine set out to do her homework, but then put off the obituary assignment by doodling in the margin of the blank page. To put something down on paper, even doodles, gave her the sense of actually having begun, having accomplished, even though she had begun nothing and had accomplished even less.

Maybe the blank page itself was the obituary.

Maxine should have handed the blank page in to her university professor.

The blank page metaphor amused me, and I chuckled,

sending a small cyclone of chuckle across the blank-page expanse of my eternity. I wondered if the thought of handing in a blank page for her obituary would have amused Maxine. Then I wondered why I didn't know if it would, if she had been dead for so long that I could have forgotten, if this disconnect was part of my being dead or part of Maxine's life. One thing I did know for certain. Even if she had thought of it, Maxine wouldn't have had the guts to hand in a blank page for her obituary assignment. She wouldn't have done it, couldn't let herself.

I felt a fleeting moment of sadness.

Perhaps it wasn't fleeting.

How am I to know with no anchor of time to measure such things?

Using a thin-point Sharpie black highlighter, Maxine had filled the margin of the rough draft of the obituary assignment with tiny gravestone markers and gothic crosses and bats and ghosts and other things of the dead. Or rather, symbols she associated with the dead in her limited knowledge, having not yet experienced dying and death firsthand, the two being very separate events and states of being. Add to her inexperience the leftovers from her little-girl church upbringing, impressions that were themselves like ghosts, since they shimmered around her for the most part unseen, rising every once in a while like mirages from the black pavement on a hot summer's day. Ghosts on the highway.

Until she was about ten, Maxine squealed anew each time she saw heat mirages on the road. Squealed as if seeing them for the very first time, a rather delightful aspect of her personality, if I may say so myself, the ability to see things afresh. There she was, leaning up from the sea of siblings in the back seat of the family car, George driving and Golda in the passenger seat, the car packed with beach paraphernalia, the afternoon frying-pan hot and sizzling. And Maxine finds magic in it, in a glimmer wavering in the distance on the black highway. It's just a mirage, Movida would say with disdain as if she were the big sister and not Maxine, quickly dismissing the ghosts on the highway and returning to her Gameboy.

It's not real, Peter would add with scientific detachment, as if Maxine didn't understand such things. Maxine wouldn't bother to argue with her brother that that was the point exactly, it wasn't real. But there it was anyway, the unreal shimmering up before her very eyes. She watched, her eyes glued to the image, careful not to blink, thinking maybe this time - maybe this time - the image wouldn't disappear, but stay put and they'd drive right into it, but it never happened. The apparition would evaporate before the car reached it, and then reappear further down the blacktop highway, and Maxine would squeal with delight and amazement afresh.

Ghosts on the highway. My memories of Maxine.

After a half hour of nothing to show for her obituary except doodles, Maxine decided to start at the beginning. It made sense. Most things began at the beginning – she would take a linear and logical approach to the obituary assignment. So she wrote her full name and date of birth across the top of the page in block letters with the Sharpie highlighter pen like this:

MAXINE LILLI-ANNE LANE
BORN MARCH 16, 1980

Maxine liked the concrete feel of a pen in her hands, wielding it, moving the writing utensil through the shape of her intentions, from her mind to the paper. In that way, she was different from the majority of her fellow journalist students, who preferred their laptops and Palm Pilots and Blackberries and cell phones to text message. Maxine wrote her first draft in longhand, started with a blank page and a pen, carried a leather journal in her bag to jot down notes and compose. Her boyfriend, Ben, would tease her, call her a throwback to another age, Lois Lane with her reporter's pen and notebook.

"Don't flatter yourself," she'd shoot back. "You're not Superman."

Maxine wasn't a complete technology Neanderthal. She transcribed her first draft notes from her journal to her laptop, used the computer to revise and polish, and then craft the final story - minus the doodles. When she was on a roll with her writing, her journal handwriting was atrocious, the thoughts coming out too fast to form anything legible. Even she had trouble deciphering what she wrote when it came time to put it in digital format.

The obituary assignment wasn't anywhere near the input-into-computer stage, still at the doodle stage of development. The doodles were part of the process, the thinking part, or rather the escape from the thinking part, the pause between the action, the re-gathering, the creative process. Or maybe the doodles didn't mean much of anything. Maybe they were just plain doodling, like so many acts in a person's life, filling in time, filling up space.

Maxine might have thought she was starting at the beginning, writing down her name and date of birth, but that really wasn't the beginning. There was conception and then nine months in her mother's womb. She didn't remember the moment of conception, possibility turned into process, the act of her becoming. I remember. Not the lovemaking, not the physical joining of Golda and George; to look upon that is taboo, even now through the window of death. Why is that? I'm no longer alive. No longer Maxine. Funny, how we never rid ourselves of parents, shed the skin of being a child, even when we're grown up and living away from home, even when we're dead and buried. It makes me wonder. If Golda showed up here, now, reborn into this otherworld, not even really Golda, since Golda was dead as Maxine is dead, would we fall into the same roles of mother and daughter? Would she tell me to pull up my collar against the cold, and would I do it, the dutiful child?

This is what I do remember: Sperm spinning through the black universe of uterus joining with the egg like the docking of two space vessels. A single cell replicating and replicating and replicating, determinedly set on a course that is Maxine, a strand of DNA stretching out into a sparkling necklace. Beads strung in exact order, the genetic code to her being. Her physical appearance, her blond hair, her brown eyes, her tendency toward being overweight, the mole on the left cheek of her behind that she preferred to call a beauty mark, the freckles spread across her face that came out in the summer like the stars in the night sky, the way her right foot turned slightly inward.

It is always present tense in the womb, no past tense, no future tense, just the moment. Golda and Maxine. Floating. No gravity, nothing to anchor them to ground, endless floating, the weightlessness of the astronaut, the umbilical cord their lifeline. The heart thundering, an immense drum, the space between each beat, both an eternity and non-existent, one beat merging with the next. The roar of the heart beat ebbing and then overwhelming. Reassuring, and intimate, and close, as close as waves crashing on a beach, your ear to the sand, water spilling over you, and then subsiding, and then spilling over you again.

As close to God as Maxine ever got.

God thundering next to her.

Maxine, and Golda, and the waves, and God.

CHAPTER 3

Birth was the first act of violence Maxine experienced, although not the last. She came into the world in an act of violence and left the world in an act of violence. There's a certain symmetry to it. There she was, warm and cosy, curled into the fetal ball, floating without knowledge of anything other than Golda's womb, water lapping over her, in rhythm with the heartbeat, primeval drumming, large and powerful. Her own heartbeat, small and gentle, joining with it. Maxine stirred slightly, shifted position, stretched her leg a bit, extended her arm, but not in discomfort. She was content.

The contraction hit her out of nowhere like a tire iron to the head. The walls of the uterus contracted violently, no small contractions first to ease her into the act of being born. Golda's muscles tightened, hard and ungiving. They pressed against Maxine with the single intent to expel her. Another contraction threw Maxine backwards, jerked her neck, and she moved her hands instinctively to her mouth, as if she intended to suck her thumb to comfort herself. But there was to be no comfort. The contractions grew in intensity, in violence. Slam dunked her like a basketball into a hoop. Thrust her down and out of the cavity that had once rocked her. Thrust her into this passageway much too narrow for her to fit. Squeezed her head where it did not want to go, so that she no longer floated in gentle suspension, but was cramped, and then smothered, the walls of the birth canal cramming against her.

Maxine felt frightened, and angry, and hurt, although she had no way of knowing that these emotions were what she felt. She fought the birth, fought the expulsion. Fought life, tried to climb back through the birth channel, back into the womb. But it doesn't work that way, the process had been put into motion. There was no returning to the womb. It was either birth or death. Golda's heartbeat slowed, the drumming fainter, and fainter, and then it stopped. The blood in her veins grew sluggish, and then thickened. The uterus grew strangely quiet. It was an eerie quiet that must have lasted only a few seconds, at the most, but hung around Maxine like an eternity.

Then garbled sounds rose from the outside. And action. A fist hammered Golda's chest. The pounding ricocheted through Maxine. Golda's heartbeat jump-started and a torrent of blood gushed through her veins in a raging river. With a single sustained contraction that on the Richter scale would have surely tipped ten, Golda gave birth. Maxine drew in a sharp breath and wailed.

✧ ✧ ✧

Some hear music and see a blinding light. They feel pulled by a presence they describe as Love. They want only to reach Love, to join with It, mingle with It. To be It. Then they die. Music, light and love. That's what Golda had described as having happened when her heart stopped beating while she gave birth to Maxine.

Dead and newly buried, without anything better to do to pass eternity, I rehashed Golda's recollections of the three-second interval between the nurse's announcement of no vital signs, and the doctor's whacking of her chest to jump-start her heart and bring her back to life. Rehashed it a thousand times, if once. I played the thought repeatedly, as if stuck in a loop in the time/space continuum. Maybe I was stuck in a loop, different rules of physics governing the otherworld.

"I died," Golda said. "The nurse couldn't find a pulse. Then I heard a choir of angels, voices more glorious than anything I have ever heard, before or after. It filled not only the room, but me, too, filled my spirit with the glory of God."

Golda told a good story, had a natural flare for the dramatic. She was the family matriarch, probably still is, having outlived her middle daughter, but still having three other children alive. She loved the dramatic and her place in the oral tradition of the family. She passed along all noteworthy news through the network of relatives and friends, embellishing the details, building to the climax, leaving the punch line to the very end. She was the hub so to speak, the centre of the wheel where all the spokes touched.

"I saw a blinding light," Golda continued. "I shielded my eyes from it, although I couldn't possibly have shielded my eyes, being dead and unable to move. But I remember moving my arms up to block the light, and when I did that, seeing a darkened figure, arms open, as if to receive me and I knew It was Jesus Christ, and I was filled with an overwhelming Love. I wanted to see the face of Christ, but a Voice said no, I couldn't look upon the face of Christ and live, and He was sending me back."

Maxine looked at her mother's face and saw disappointment. Golda hadn't wanted to return to her body. Hadn't wanted to leave overwhelming Love. Hadn't wanted the doctor to resuscitate her with that one hard punch to the chest.

"Why do you think He sent me back?" she asked.

Golda seemed truly perplexed. Why had she been saved?

She hadn't gone to India to become a missionary and turn the atheistic little Buddha-children to Christianity, she hadn't been resurrected with the sudden ability to heal or read minds or turn on light bulbs simply by touching them, she hadn't received the gift of song, rendering beautifully the praises of God. She hadn't given birth to the next Saviour, or the first woman astronaut to walk on the moon, or a great movie star, or a famous news anchor.

She had given birth to Maxine.

The ways of the Lord are, indeed, mysterious.

Golda had wanted Maxine to be a television news anchor.

"You'd be good at it," she encouraged her daughter. "You're pretty, and you're smart, and you have a wonderful smile and a good speaking voice."

It was true. Maxine was pretty and smart, and she did have a wonderful smile and a good speaking voice. But she didn't want to be a television news anchor. The idea of standing in front of a camera, her image sent live to a million people at a sitting, terrified her.

"You might have to start with the weather," Golda said, "but you'd advance fast. Be doing the news in no time. Imagine it! Sent to exotic places to cover warfare, and terrorists, and coronations, and hostage takings, and presidential elections, and natural disasters, and sniper attacks, and airplane hijackings."

Golda sighed with the glorious joy of her daughter in the thick of the action.

"Those places would be dangerous!" Maxine exclaimed. "You'd send me into a hale of gunfire to fulfill your dream of my being a broadcaster?"

"Yes," Golda said. "Anyway, what guarantees are there in life? You might be killed by a drunk driver. Murdered in a drive-by shooting. Raped and left naked to die at the side of the highway. Ravaged at an early age by ovarian cancer. Decapitated by—"

"Thanks!" Maxine said.

"You're welcome," Golda answered, turning on the evening news.

Maxine admired her mother's hmmfff. Her "grab the world by the balls" and "go get it" attitude. She thought that if Golda hadn't married so young and had a family so fast, she'd probably be the ambassador to France. Or Prime Minister of Canada, or the female version of Billy Graham, or the lead anchor of CNN. Or the founder and head psychic of the Psychics Telephone Hotline, or a new age faith healer with a world-wide cult following, or a television broadcaster on assignment in exotic and dangerous locales. Bullets routinely whizzing by her head.

Maxine compromised. Became a print journalist.

Anyway, she liked words. Words were easier than television cameras. She could hide behind them. They provided a buffer between Life, and her life.

✧ ✧ ✧

So there I was, dead and newly buried, and thinking about Golda. In her single lifetime, she had experienced speaking-in-tongues, slaying-in-the-spirit, ghost sightings, psychic premonitions, miracle healings and messages from the dead. And to top it all off, her near-death experience.

Why had Maxine's death been so different from Golda's near-death experience? No light show, no music, no God-sighting accompanied Maxine's eternal send-off. I tried to rationalize the fact. I thought maybe Maxine hadn't been good enough, or caring enough, or prayed enough, or shown enough faith, or accomplished the required number of good deeds. Maybe good deeds were tallied, and Maxine had fallen one deed short, or maybe Golda's near-death visions had no concrete reality of their own, but were simply a by-product of chemicals. Maybe it was something Golda had eaten that day, or her brain shutting down, in the same way aerobic exercise shoots endorphins into the system to induce a natural high. Maxine once read in a book called *The Secret Life of Plants* that trees went into a coma when they were about to be chopped. It was a self-induced drugging to deal with their impending deaths.

Maxine had done the same, after the first blow from the tire iron.

The night was deep black, the fog lifting and then dropping like breath, the road bending so that she almost ran off the edge. No other traffic, no gas stations, no houses, just the forest and the mist and the thick night. Maxine hadn't passed any cars for at least a half hour, not since she had driven through Pembroke. She turned on the high beams, and then suddenly, another car, off to the side of the road, the hood lifted in the universal sign of trouble. And the man beside the car, his face caught in the headlights, his expression unreadable. Then that moment of indecision where everything hangs in the balance. Should she stop or not?

Maxine drove by, fifty metres or so down the highway, then thought better of it, or worse, pulled off to the shoulder, put her car into reverse, backed up.

She rolled down the window.

"Do you want me to call a tow truck?" she asked, reaching for her cell.

"Sure," he said, as if he meant it, and then he smiled, a charming smile. "You know, don't bother – do you have cables? If you could just give me a boost, that would be a godsend, my car battery is dead."

Maxine did have cables.

In the trunk. Ben had put them there. Just in case.

She got out of the car.

Walked around to the back.

Opened the trunk, turned to face the man with the charming smile, her car keys still in her hand. Didn't get completely turned around, caught a glimpse of the tire iron held above his head. She felt the blow, an excruciating burning like a branding, and fell, her face slamming against the shoulder, her keys clattering across the highway. She blacked out before the next blow. Unconsciousness closed over her, mixed with the night. No bright light opened up a passageway to the otherworld. Her last sensations were of fog, and the grit of stone in her mouth, and the beginning taste of blood, sickly sweet, and the unbearable stinging across the side of her face, and then blackness.

CHAPTER 4

Do unto others as you'd want them to do unto you. Teachings of compassion, instilled in Maxine from an early age, made Golda an accomplice to murder of sorts. Oh, Golda wasn't at the side of the road that treacherous night, didn't personally swing the tire iron. She loved Maxine dearly, would never wish her harm. Golda would have done everything in her power to save her daughter, switched places with her, if the universe worked that way, if she could have struck a bargain with God, with the devil, with the angel of death, whomever is the Cosmic Bargain Striker. But it's not fair to place the greater share of the compassion-blame on Golda. Society teaches little girls to fulfill the helping roles, to be the nurse, the teacher, the nurturer, to be givers, not takers.

Consider the night of Maxine's death. There she is, driving a dark stretch of highway between Pembroke and Petawawa in northern Ontario. At exactly eleven minutes past eleven, she sees a car at the shoulder of the road, hood up in the universal sign of distress. Maxine hesitates. By nature, she is reticent. But the genetic code is complex, and by nature, Maxine is also compassionate. Then throw in a big dose of nurture. The two attributes, reticence and compassion, reinforced by nurture, egged on by nurture, played themselves out in different concentrations throughout Maxine's life. Sometimes reticence won out, and she would say nothing, take no action. Sometimes compassion won out, and she would be moved to act.

On her final night, compassion won out.

Maxine hesitated, then acted.

She stopped to help.

But then Maxine wasn't the first woman to be killed responding to a plea for help, and neither will she be the last.

Compassion is a common killer.

✧ ✧ ✧

Maxine's first encounter with the demand for feminine compassion came at an early age. At least, it was the first encounter she remembered that made a conscious imprint upon her impressionable child's brain. Golda had dressed Maxine in a pink-and-white gingham sunsuit, a bonnet with a giant brim, white ankle socks, and those little white shoes that babies wear. She tied a bell through each of the laces so that Maxine tinkled when she toddled. Then they went to the park, Adeline pushing her doll in a carriage, Peter riding a tricycle, Maxine being pushed in a stroller by Golda, Movida along for the ride, still in Golda's tummy.

The park was two blocks away, quite an adventure, quite a distance for Golda and her family. In mother-duck fashion they arrived, a feat in itself, having negotiated a busy street corner, a car whizzing by Adeline, missing the little girl by inches and causing her to cry.

On a grassy stretch of park, Golda spread out the blanket, then set Maxine on it and gave her a teething biscuit to munch. Then she gave Peter a pail and a shovel, and set him in the sandbox to play. She set Adeline in the direction of the swings, and then set herself down on the blanket with Maxine. Everything "set" just right, she opened a canned drink and gave

herself, and therefore Movida in her tummy, a drink.
A little boy grabbed for Maxine's biscuit.
Maxine pulled her hand away. It was her biscuit. Not his.

The boy was a giant by Maxine's standards, large and pudgy, strawberry ice cream remnants staining his face and shirt and fingers. He pouted, his mouth dropping downward and his bottom lip jutting. But Maxine did not second-guess herself. In her eighteen-month-old mind, she was decisive and certain and justified. She *would not* let him take the biscuit.

"Mine!" she said, the possessive newly entrenched in her vocabulary.

It was ingrained in her now, this viewpoint of self and others, this separation of the world into distinct entities. She intended to fight to protect what was hers, whether a cookie or her life.

Retribution was unexpected and swift.

"Bad girl!" Golda's mother scolded.

She snatched Maxine's half-eaten biscuit, gummy and wet, and tossed it into a big wire garbage container. Then she did the unthinkable, the perplexing. She handed the boy a clean new biscuit from the box. Maxine waited for her clean new biscuit, held out her hand, then cried for one. Golda opened up her *Woman's World* and read, didn't look in her direction, ignored the crying.

Maxine continued to cry, now more for her mother's attention than for the biscuit. It was similar to the time she learned to eat prunes, not because she liked them, but for Golda's approval. Golda had stirred the prunes into a mush, added a pinch of sugar for taste, and then made faces. Maxine learned to laugh at her mother's facial contortions not because they were funny, but because she picked up the cues that she was supposed to laugh. Singular attention is a rare commodity in a large family and she acted to prolong it, even if the price were prunes dropped into the cavity of her smile.

When Maxine was a child, she felt compassion for everything around her. Too much compassion at times, since she would even cry for make-believe characters. An example was Tinkerbelle in *Peter Pan*, when the children in TV land were asked to clap for the little fairy to give her the strength to live.

Her brother Peter would yell, "Die Tinkerbelle! Die!"

Maxine would scream at him to stop and then sob a river, although she had watched the movie at least ten times and never once had it deviated from the happy ending.

Tinkerbelle always *lived*.

Maxine's compassion for all things living led her to hold funerals for all things dead. She scoured the grass for dead grasshoppers and the windowsills for dead houseflies. When a body was found, she gathered together the neighbourhood children to give the insect a proper burial. The ceremonies were elaborate and soulful. Hymns and eulogies and tears and a matchbox coffin. A burial plot, earth raised into a mound, edged by tiny stones, carefully gathered and laid to rest in a circle around the dirt. A bluebell or a petunia or a lilac taken from the garden according to season.

Maxine did not tolerate disrespect. She swiftly scolded any child who giggled during the ceremony, which ultimately meant almost everyone in the neighbourhood at some time or another. Her best friend Becky alone recognized the solemnity of the occasion. She understood Maxine's sorrow and cried real tears with her. Not even Maxine's own sisters did as much. Movida, in her exuberance and love of the theatrical, killed the bugs with her own hands in order to prompt a funeral.

"But they were going to die someday. I just helped them along," she protested when Maxine finally figured out why Movida found five times more dead bugs than anyone else.

Maxine accused her younger sister of murder.

Firstborn sibling Adeline vigorously came to Movida's defense, arguing bugs did not have souls and therefore did not go to heaven. It was a waste of time to hold a funeral for them, an abomination, really. God Himself would disapprove, since insects, especially houseflies, were soul-less and were meant to rot in the very spot where they died, as they should, in keeping with the Divine Laws. "And anyway," Adeline added, before she and Movida left hand-in-hand to go to the corner store to buy a Popsicle, "who died and put you in charge?"

Golda watched the funeral services from the window. She carefully peeked out from behind the curtain, not wanting to disturb the proceedings. Golda smiled to herself at how nicely Maxine was growing up, and held in her heart the memory of her daughter's compassion.

Maxine's brother Peter took pot shots at the funeral party from a distance.

He spit white peas from his lime green peashooter. Some of the peas landed in the soil stacked against the garage and grew into tiny pea plants, a living monument to how the universe works. One entity's actions (in this case, pea-spitting by a skinny, knee-scraped spit of an Earth boy named Peter) fulfilled a notably different role from that which spurred the action in the first place.

Maybe it was the same for Maxine's short life.

Maybe she fulfilled a notably different role than I have fathomed.

Or maybe that's purely wishful thinking; in the end, we all want to think our lives are worth it.

✧ ✧ ✧

Then there's religion.

Jesus, Buddha, Mohammad: three male teachers, each twisting his own version of the Golden Rule. A follower of Christ puts it in the affirmative: Do unto others as you would want them to do unto you. A Buddhist negatively: Hurt not others in ways you yourself would find hurtful. And the Muslim: No one is a believer until you desire for another that which you desire for yourselves. The Jew will preach it too: What is hateful to you do not do to your neighbour. That is the entire Torah. The rest is commentary.

The others are no less guilty, even the ancient ones.

Zoroastrianism: Human nature is good only when it does not do unto another whatsoever is not good for its own self. Jainism: In happiness and suffering, in joy and grief, regard all creatures as you would your own self. The Bahai: Blessed are those who prefer others before themselves. Variations in style, but the message is the same. Be kind to others, serve patiently, give of yourself without distrust. In practical application, stop at the side of the road in the middle of the night to help the man in distress.

Of course, you do have to place blame where it belongs, squarely on the shoulders of the man who preyed on Maxine's compassion, counted on the odds that she'd Golden-Rule it. And if not this young woman, if not Maxine alone and rounding the highway's bend, foot easing off the gas pedal, hands steering car to the side of the road, slipping clutch into reverse, edging back along the shoulder, tires crunching on gravel, eyes to the rear view mirror, image of the man who would be her death, reflected double in her pupils, as black and large as the night – then another young woman.

✧ ✧ ✧

Step on a crack, break your mother's back. If Golda tried to protect Maxine, as best she could and then some, the two of them joined in that invisible way called love, Maxine also tried to protect Golda, as best she could and then some. When Maxi skipped just right, kept the spring in her step just so, she missed the cracks that appeared with the regularity of clockwork in the sidewalk, the cracks that stretched in front of her for an eternity, like a railroad track disappearing into the horizon. But when she changed her gait, the spread of her step, then she risked stepping on the crack, breaking her mother's back.

It was a big responsibility, being responsible for your mother's well-being. The little girl took it seriously. When Maxi miscalculated her step, as happened every once upon a time, and her tiny foot went smack dab across the crack, she would go home fearfully, creeping into the house to see if Golda were hurt. If she lay broken on the linoleum of the kitchen floor, the black and red tiles like a giant checkerboard.

Once when she played the skipping game, which really wasn't a game at all since her mother's back depended upon it, Maxi tripped on her untied shoelace and fell. She hit the sidewalk and scraped her knee. Blood trickled down her leg and stained her white ankle sock. She cried at the stinging pain, but just as much she cried at the violence committed against her by the sidewalk. Then her cries grew larger than that, larger than just a matter of a sidewalk and a little girl's bleeding knee. She cried at the sum total of all the violence she would suffer, that she could hurt, that she could bleed. And in her little girl way, she understood that this God awe-full truth was the way of the universe.

At other times, just being alive made Maxi feel joyful.

She couldn't voice the thought, put it into words, too young, the whole thing more of a feeling, an experience. On one such day, she had just discovered that she could go out into the sun all by herself, dance on the front lawn all by herself, push her bare feet into the cool grass, spin on her toes, the hem of her dress swirling around her knees, wide in a circle, so that she was a flower, petals wide-open to the sun. She could push open the screen door, push hard with both hands, didn't need her mother or father, or her big sister or brother, and if she could open the screen door, dance on the grass by herself, then she could also cross the road, visit Mrs. Abbott who might give her a chocolate.

Maxi stepped out on the sparkling black road.

At first step, at the first sign of pain, the little girl didn't think to turn around, to return to the cool grass of her front yard, as if once embarked upon the journey there was no turning back, only going forward to the other side. So Maxi sprinted across the road and sat down on Mrs. Abbott's lawn. She sat with her knees pushed outward and her ankles close to her body, in lotus position almost, so that her soles did not touch the ground. She didn't know what to do. The hot tar had burnt her feet raw. Her feet were red and blistering and they hurt. She couldn't walk. She could crawl like a baby, but that would mean crossing the road again. She started to wail as if she had the weight of the world, the universe, the cosmos, on her tiny shoulders. And she did, in a sense, if everything is relative. If each incident can be judged against its own particular situation, and not solely against some Almighty Absolute, against which nothing can be judged worthy or significant or valid.

Golda appeared suddenly like an angel.

She swept Maxi into her arms, comforted her, wiped her tears, held her close. Carried her home in such a way that Maxi's legs dangled and her feet did not touch the black tar, did not touch the sidewalk or the porch steps or anything else that might hurt them. Golda brushed ointment on Maxi's feet. The ointment and Golda's soft clucking and tender touch soothed the little girl, made her almost forget, made the pain almost go away, but not quite.

Never quite.

CHAPTER 5

After writing her name and date of birth across the top of her obituary assignment page, Maxine sketched a casket with a dead girl lying inside, her fingers linked in peaceful repose across her chest. She made the dead girl's hair long and straight, somewhat like her own hair, and put a necklace around the dead girl's neck, one simple piece of jewellery. It was not a crucifix as one might expect on a line drawing of a dead girl. The dead girl wore a chain with a Buddha charm dangling from it, similar to the one that Maxine wore at the moment of the obituary assignment.

It might have been déjà vu, the doodling, that Maxine had a vision of her own premature death, had tapped into the psychic stream. After all, my hands were crossed in the same manner as the obituary drawing when I woke up in the coffin, although I suppose that isn't a dependable indication of anything other than I am dead, that Maxine did indeed die, and that the undertaker laid her body out in the usual custom. And the long hair, well, Maxine's hair was blond and the sketching of the dead girl had vampire black, although the Sharpie thin-point highlighter was black, so the choice of colour may have been one of necessity, rather than clairvoyance. And the vampire black suited the theme, Maxine having half-joked with Ben a series of obituary assignment one-liners, like "yeah, drive a stake through my heart, why don't you?" when he offered to read the day's obituaries from the *Ottawa Citizen* to her in bed that night. And then she added, "That sounds romantic – why don't you just save the bother and kill me now?"

"Some people get off on that kind of thing," Ben responded.

"Get off on what?"

"Death."

"People get off on death?"

"Yeah, or the flirting with death. They cut off the air-supply. Of course, they have to ensure someone trustworthy is around to loosen the noose before it's too late."

"That would be important," Maxine quipped.

It's always better to have someone around to save you from death.

"The theory is you're never so purely alive as the moment before you die. Sensation is heightened. The trick is - if you can call playing with death a trick - to get closer and closer to that point of no return, but be pulled back from it at the last possible moment, like yanking up a yo-yo."

"Walk the Dog. The Sleeper."

Perfect. The Sleeper. The Big Sleep.

"What?" Ben asked.

"They're yo-yo tricks. In the Sleeper, you throw the yo-yo like this," Maxine said, miming the action, exaggerating it in a bigger-than-life way. "When the string is fully-extended, at the very end of its rope, the yo-yo spins there, doesn't roll back up. You let it sleep like that, and at the last possible moment, you pull it back up into your hand."

Maxine drew a yo-yo in the margin beside the coffin with the vampire girl. Drew the string from the very top of the page down to the very bottom of the page. Put little lines around the yo-yo like giant quotation marks to show the spinning.

"Do you think it's true?" Maxine asked Ben.

"What's that?"

"That you're never so alive as the moment you die?"
The first trickling of the sweet-sick taste of blood.
Night death black.
Mist arising from the marshlands like spirit slipping away.
Ghosts on the highway.

✧   ✧   ✧

It's pretty safe to say that Maxine's sketching of a coffin, and a dead girl with long hair like her own, wearing a Buddha chain like her own, drawn on the side of her obituary, wasn't clairvoyance. It was a random act of coincidence, two unrelated events that accidentally coincide, or collide, like atoms in a nuclear explosion.

Cosmic irony.

If it had been an actual premonition, Maxine would have been buried with the Buddha charm around her neck as she had drawn it on the obituary assignment, and I'd be wearing it right now. But the necklace hadn't made the trip to the otherworld; it certainly hadn't been sent with me as a goodbye gesture by Adeline or Golda, along with the other paraphernalia they had felt spiritually fit to stuff into my coffin, the Palm Sunday palm branch from Sunday school days, pressed flat in Adeline's Bible, and the vial of holy water from the River Jordan that Golda had bought on sale at Agape Christian bookstore. Nor had the necklace slipped off Maxine's neck and fallen lost in the waves of the peach-coloured satin lining, jarred undone when the pallbearers carried Maxine's body from the hearse to the gravesite, or the cemetery contraption lowered her six-feet down into the ground.

It wasn't there. Period.
I should know.

✧ ✧ ✧

The otherworld is an underground.

I don't call this place where I find myself the afterlife, since there was first life and then death, and now this unexpected world after death, this other world.

I describe it as an underground, because I am still part Maxine.

Maxine was a journalist. Journalists think about words and try to choose the right ones. I guess you can shuck off your body, but you can't completely shuck off who you were. It sticks to you, as if the stuff of the soul - although I don't know if it is the soul, if there is such a thing. A common misconception, that death brings absolute knowledge.

The otherworld is not an underground in the sense you might expect, in a six-feet-under kind of way, where you're put in a box and the lid shuts, and the earth closes above you, and you scream *open the goddamn box*, but no one does because they can't hear you, you're dead. Granted, it started like that - there I was, lying on my back, hands folded, wearing mortality like a straitjacket, the physical body refusing to respond, my demands soon sinking into plea-bargaining and panic. Please let me live, I'll be good, I'll go to church. I'll abstain from sex, become a missionary, dedicate my life to saving the planet; my God, I can't be dead, why me, Lord? It is all you know, corporeal existence, and your first reaction is to cling to it, cling to life, your death as fresh as a newborn.

But being dead and six feet under is not the reason for my description of the otherworld as an underground. The source of that statement comes from a visit to Elliott Lake in Northern Ontario. When Maxine was full of life and equally full of questions, she had quizzed her friend, Joel, about working in the uranium mines. To Joel, who was a miner and not a journalist, mere words were a pale substitute for the real thing, so he took her on a tour to show her firsthand what it was like to go underground. Maxine put on a hard hat and overalls, as required by the uranium mine officials, not that she minded. It was part of the adventure, part of the ride. The get-up made her feel blue collar-ish, as if she herself could work the mines or fix an engine or fell a tree. Writers have vivid imaginations.

Maxine stepped into a very large elevator that took her underground, not six feet, but a mile below the surface. The elevator, which was really only a square metal box on a pulley, sank through walls of rock. Maxine began to fear for her life, the movement jerking before settling into a constant speed. She had no way of knowing that she needn't be concerned, that she wouldn't plunge to her death in a elevator shaft, that an unexpected earthquake wouldn't spill megatons of uranium-plundered stone to crush her skull. Maxine still had three, almost four years of life left in her.

Maxine also learned something new about herself.

She was claustrophobic.

Sinking through solid rock, there was no escape. She just had to hang on for the ride. She could do absolutely nothing to combat the claustrophobia, except panic, and she would never let herself do that. She didn't like to show fear, what she was really feeling. It was an inherited quality. A stubbornness residing in a specific gene passed along from her prairie grandmother and integral to prairie survival.

Down Maxine went, deeper and deeper, completely encased in rock and entombed before her time. Sun and sky existed only as memory, if objects do indeed exist as memory. It is a question I sometimes ponder, a pale comparison of my former self, a pale substitute to the real thing, here with my memories.

The elevator stopped, and everyone clambered out in their hard hats and overalls. Maxine followed Joel down a tunnel that opened into a large chamber. She smiled at him, masking the panic at the mile of rock above her. The room was the size of a gymnasium and held large machinery and trucks. She hadn't expected machinery this big. They must have assembled it underground, she thought.

Maxine licked her lips. She realized for the first time that air had substance.

In comparison, the atmosphere underground was thin.

Air aboveground pressed around you like a thick blanket.

Why hadn't she this noticed before?

Maxine yearned to breathe aboveground air, to take it far inside of her, at a molecular level into her cells. And that is what I mean. Why I say it is an underground, this otherworld. Sometimes I yearn for sensation again, the earthly senses pressing on me like a thick blanket, the heaviness of smell and sound and taste and touch and sight, the overwhelming tangibility of life, the weight of atmosphere.

CHAPTER 6

I don't know in earth-time how long I lay there, waiting for some action to take place, waiting for devil or God to appear, angel or Buddha, heaven or hell, whether a split second had passed or an eternity. But Satan did not show up, nor did Jesus, decked out in flowing purple robes and a crown, thorns or otherwise. My guardian angel did not make an appearance, nor Buddha, at least not while I was in my coffin.

By now, I was bored to death with death. I scanned the lid for a pinprick of holy light, but none shone through the coffin. It was air-tight, light-tight, water-tight, maggot tight, all designed to keep Maxine's body intact and safe from the elements. Solid hard wood, high-gloss lacquer, reddish tint to the grain, some poor cherry tree had given its life. Metal screws holding together my Fort Knox of coffins, no wooden dowels or environmentally friendly glue here. Golda and George had spared no expense, I wished they had spared some expense, at least a bit, well, spared a lot. I wished they had thought green, left Maxine's body as an environmental legacy, hurried along the decay, left me some biodegradable escape hatch. A cardboard box, made of 100% naturally hardened recycled paper, or a casket woven of all-natural materials - willow, wicker, bamboo, even banana leaves, for God's sake, for Earth's sake, for my sake, for Maxine's sake. Less guilt, less sin, less to account for at the pearly gates, carbon footprint reduced in death, adding to the good of the planet rather than taking away from it.

I strained my ears for music, and opened my heart to Love. I waited. No light, no Love. Nothing. I felt defeat. Gave up hope of resurrection. But then I heard a faint sound, the sweet voices of angels. The sound gained strength, and I rejoiced. What music did God download when He came to quicken the dead? Surely Mozart or Beethoven or Bach, the Goldberg Variations performed by Glenn Gould, orchestral and instrumentally heavenly, creatively complicated, divine fingers running over the ivories in a rush of glory.

You wish.

I wish.

A guitar whined from somewhere outside the coffin, the annoying electric-saw buzz of a mosquito on a hot summer's night. The whining grew louder, one big bloodsucker of a sound, a giant vampire mosquito outside my casket. Just when I thought this was hell, the guitar switched to vocals, a brooding soft voice without discernible words, a sadness floating on it, the vulnerability of a dandelion seed on the water's surface. It was hauntingly mournful, hauntingly beautiful in a morbid way, love lost, and I thought I might cry, but I didn't.

Then finally something happened, glory be to God Almighty, King of the heavenly hosts, and whatever else they taught Maxine in Sunday school. The cosmos appeared above me, stars and suns and moons and blackness, like the roof of a planetarium. I regretted that Maxine hadn't paid more attention to the stars when she was alive. How gloriously gratefully time-consuming it would be to name each of the constellations that spread before my eyes. I searched for the Big Dipper, the extent of my star-knowledge. Then a shooting star exploded across my field of vision, a meteor really, if I were to be technical. The star-meteor grew in magnitude, took on the definition of shape until I recognized it was neither star nor meteor. To be truly technical, it was a door, ornate and finely carved, Victorian era, elaborate curlicues. As the door drew closer, the carvings, too, were magnified, took on shape and meaning, bats with wings outstretched, some large and some small - mini bats - the cosmos playing word games with me. There were dancing ghost girls, arms linked like paper dolls, and gravestones and large crosses and dead girls in coffins, carvings flowing into each other, interlocked like Escher drawings, demons and angels, bats and ghosts, a Goth door.

The strangest things cross your mind at the strangest times, and you wonder later, why did I think that? I didn't question the fact that the cosmos had suddenly spread above me, nor that this Edgar-Allen-Poe door had appeared in the midst of the stars. Neither did I question what would happen next, or why things had changed at this moment when they had remained the same for so long. Instead, I thought, "Probably the door is locked."

But then the door swung open, and the melancholy ballad-dirge morphed into the mad frenzied blaring of a rock concert. A single refrain repeated itself over and over and over, a classic from the rock band of rock bands, the mother of New Wave and punk and Goth and death rock, one leading to the other like action reaction if you're an Einstein freak, like evolution if you're a Darwin freak.

Jim Morrison of The Doors singing *Break on through to the other side*.

Miraculously, without thinking about the dangers or the consequences, whether the door held eternal damnation or eternal bliss, I got up and left my coffin. Seeped through the thick wood lid, through the six feet of dirt, through the atmosphere, through the hole in the ozone layer, through the cosmos, toward the door, through the open door. On the other side, I caught sight of God, or the God-principle, or Whatever. He played a bitchin' guitar and had long hair and bounced up and down like a raving maniac. Death rock rocked the cosmos, the stars and suns and the moons reverberating with the music of the spheres. God looked strangely like Tom Cruise playing Lestat in the movie, *Interview with a Vampire*. White silk shirt, ruffles around the neck and sticking out from his jacket sleeves, the black velvet jacket long and tailored in a Renaissance Fair kind of way, his trousers neatly ironed with a crease that could draw blood. Then another ridiculous, absolutely wrong-for-the-moment thought: who irons God's pants?

Before I could ask, He evaporated.

I think there's a point to be made here. It goes like this: You can't stick around waiting for things to happen to you.
You can't sit around waiting for redemption, or revelation, or the Second Coming. You've got to take the initiative. Pull yourself up out of your coffin and go meet whatever head on.

CHAPTER 7

Action and reticence. Sometimes Maxine hung back, watched. Other times she acted decisively, demonstrated bravery if not foolhardiness for her personal safety. On these latter occasions, compassion was the deciding factor, emphatically tipping the scale with a solid thud, moving her to act.

Reticence, like compassion, came to Maxine early in life.

Golda and Peter spent the day in question fussing over Maxine's hand-me-down doll carriage. They scrubbed the rust off the handle and the screws that held the handle in place with steel wool. They shone the spokes until they sparkled. They washed dirt off the underbelly and sides. They touched up the scratches with paint from an abandoned paint-by-number set. They tightened the wobbly wheels and dripped oil on them so they didn't creak.

This attention to her doll carriage struck young Maxine as novel, if not odd. Peter never wanted to play with her or her toys. Golda seldom played, too busy keeping everybody fed and washed and out of trouble. The attention continued throughout the day and into the early evening.

Then came the strangest behaviour of all.

Behaviour that delighted Maxine.

Golda tore toilet paper into squares and crafted flowers. She gently spread apart the tissue to create petals. She smudged red lipstick on the petals and sprayed the flowers with her Ode de Paris cologne. She taped the flowers onto the carriage to form a paper rose garden brimming with scented blooms. Golda laughed, a joyful sound that Maxine put inside her heart and remembered always.

Maxine's father, George, arrived home from his shift at the factory and set down his lunch bucket to untie his work boots. Before he could straighten his back, little Maxi reached up to grab his finger and pulled him to see her doll carriage. He didn't say a word, just made a long slow whistle noise.

Then he picked Maxine up beneath her underarms and tossed her high into the air. For a single moment, Maxine was suspended above everyone else, that exact moment when she was neither ascending or descending, the very peak of the toss. And in that split second, that tiny slice of time, life was perfect. It was one of those moments, maybe *the* moment that, in hindsight, makes a life worth living. There was Maxine, flying. Her father's arms outstretched, ready to catch her. The moment joyously, gloriously, frozen there for all eternity, the conservation of energy, nothing destroyed.

The next morning Golda roused Maxine from bed early.

"Hurry," she said, her voice rushed.

She dressed the little girl in a pretty summer church dress, brushed her hair, and put a shiny pink ribbon in it. Peter got his own cereal, and stood impatiently at the door. "Hurry," he said. "We'll be late."

Along the way, Maxine noticed other children and their doll carriages, too. Beautiful doll carriages decorated with streamers and sparkles and glitters and ribbons and bows. By the time the family reached the park, a parade of doll carriages had gathered. And a parade of children. And a parade of families.

Excitement hung in the air.

Maxine noticed a new feeling. It gathered like a rubber ball in the pit of her stomach. An unpleasant feeling. A lack of confidence perhaps, or a shyness, or maybe a feeling borne from a fear of failure, or disappointing others, or disappointing herself. All she knew is that she wanted to hide. Rather, she wanted to be hidden. Passive form. She moved behind Golda's legs, peered between them. Golda took hold of Maxine, pulled her out from behind her legs and pushed her forward.

The children were arranged in rows, each child standing behind a decorated carriage. The organizers of the event put Maxine in the middle of the third row.

"Move to the front," Golda coached from the sidelines. "They can't see you there."

Maxine stood rooted to her spot.

The unpleasant sensation stayed with her, along with the desire to hide.

She did not move to the front.

Stayed right where she was, smack dab middle-of-the-row.

"Go on," Golda urged louder. "Move up."

The judges huddled and talked in hushed tones. They made marks on clipboards. Then they made a big show of putting a fancy red ribbon on one of the carriages. They walked right by Maxine and then put ribbons on two more carriages. The crowd clapped. The carriages and children dispersed.

"Why didn't you move to the front?" Golda said, a statement of fact rather than a question. "You would have won a ribbon, too."

Maxine didn't know the words to form an answer.

But words or not, reticence had taken root.

✧ ✧ ✧

An August day, her eighth summer: If not the birth of action overcoming reticence, then a very good example of it, a case-in-point. Maxine had no reason to believe that this particular day would be any different from the month of past summer days. She walked barefoot. Her soles were tarpaper tough from the month of holidays and shoeless walking, unlike when she was a toddler and the pavement had burned her soft feet. Now, she could trek across roads and even stones without feeling discomfort.

Maxine's hair swung long and loose, bleached by the sun, bangs hanging in her eyes. Her skin was dark, tanned from the long days spent at the docks a few blocks from her house. She left for the docks early in the morning, only leaving reluctantly for supper at her mother's insistence. She took a packed lunch with her, and a large beach towel, wore her bathing suit under a long oversized t-shirt.

"You'll turn into a water rat," Golda would say, only half-joking.

Maxine's family lived in a white stucco house on top of a hill. When Maxine stepped out of the vestibule, took two giant steps to the sidewalk, then turned south, one quarter rotation of her body, she could see the St. Lawrence River. Every day, from the time she was a little girl riding a rusty hand-me-down tricycle, stretching her legs to reach the block pedals and turn the wheels, right up until the day thirteen years later when she packed and left home for university, she had seen the river, unconsciously noted its shades and moods. Whether the river was choppy, white caps cresting and then collapsing, whether the river was calm, flat and undisturbed as the mirror that hung in her bedroom. The freeze up in the early winter, the rush of the cargo ships to escape the Seaway before the ice caught them, the open channel a dark strip until it, too, was solid. The fierce break-up in the spring, the rush of water loosening, ice jamming and heaving, the boulders crushing up against each other, up against the docks.

Maxine lived at the edge of a river her whole life, first the St. Lawrence and then the Ottawa, was never without river. The presence of river was one of those unconscious knowings, a flowing in the background of her existence like an underlying theme. None of her brothers and sisters felt the same affinity to the river, nor did her father George, a prairie boy who never learned to swim until he moved to Ontario, and even then swam like he was trying to climb out of the water, to get on top if it, his chest and head and chin held high, his lips pierced together, his hands moving as if to part the Dead Sea, to push the water away. Maxine's brother Peter spent his summers on the baseball field and might dive into the river for a quick dip to cool off between games. Baby sister Movida preferred the sand, building castles shaped by her pail and discarded cups and Margarine containers, edging the turrets with scallops made with her shovel, digging winding moats and irrigation systems. Older sister Adeline avoided the river, smeared on dollops of sunscreen so she wouldn't get skin cancer, hated the smell and feel of the seaweed that collected at the shoreline, squealed at the sight of dead perch belly exposed and arched, white underside and orange spot like an egg cooked sunny-side up.

Although George and Golda occasionally packed their children into the car on a sticky-hot weekend for an outing to the provincial beach twelve kilometres upriver along the highway, only Maxine walked the short distance to the docks every day during the summer. The water was deep, and there was no beach or gradual sloping of the river bottom. The place where Maxine swam was actually a cement-and-steel shoring of the water's edge where in past days the luxury cabin cruisers and sailboats of the rich docked when touring the Thousand Islands. There were no lifeguards to keep order and a sense of frontier prevailed, the Wild West.

On this day, a circle of boys tossed a ball as Maxine approached the docks. They hooted and hollered, exuberantly for an ordinary game of catch. Then Maxine saw that the ball was not a ball at all, but a kitten. Without thought for her own safety, Maxine ran to close the gap. Now, in their midst, she felt the desire to run and hide, but stood ground, grabbed for the kitten. Shoved from behind, Maxine fell flat on the ground, and in an uncharacteristic act of aggression, bit the nearest ankle. "You want the fucking kitten, then go get it," a boy yelped, and shot-putted the ball of fur into the river.

Maxine belly-flopped off the end of the dock and swam to where the kitten struggled to stay afloat. She struggled herself, grabbing the kitten, holding it above the water, kicking to stay at the surface, using her free hand to paddle toward the ladder, to pull herself up onto the dock.

The kitten's fur clung to its body so that it looked like a drenched water rat. Maxine wrapped the kitten in her red beach towel, clutched kitten and towel, and went home, straight to her bedroom, right past Golda sitting in the living room and crocheting granny squares as she watched her late afternoon soaps.

In her bedroom, on her bed covered with a granny-square quilt made by Golda, Maxine carefully unwrapped the beach towel. The tiny animal pulled up on shaky legs, meowed plaintively, nuzzled its head against Maxine's wrist.

Golda entered without knocking, looked at her daughter, looked at the kitten, didn't say a word, didn't tell Maxine that the kitten was too thin, too young, too weak. She simply left the room and returned with a small bowl of warm milk.

The kitten licked three times at the milk, its tongue pink and velvet.

"Drink Juliet," Maxine whispered.

Maxine called the kitten Juliet because it was the prettiest name she could imagine. She hadn't yet read the Shakespearian tragedy, didn't know that Juliet was the name of the doomed.

Golda heard Maxine call the kitten Juliet, and in the whispering of a name, knew that the two had bonded, that they were joined in an invisible way as strong as love. There was nothing Golda could do about it now. Nothing. She left the room, shutting the door softly behind her.

The next morning, Maxine woke early, full of anticipation, the kitten asleep on the pillow beside her. "Rise and shine, Juliet," she said.

But the kitten did not rise, did not shine.

"It's not fair," Maxine yelled, pounding her fists against Golda.

Golda held her daughter, smothered her face against her bosom. The little girl felt small and helpless against the geography of her mother, against the geography of how things *were.* "It's not fair," she repeated. "I rescued the kitten from the boys, and she still died."

"Life's not fair," Golda said.

She stroked Maxine's hair. "But don't worry, take heart. The kitty's in kitty heaven, chasing mice, having a lovely time."

Maxine pushed her mother away.

"That's stupid," she said. "Kitty heaven. What kind of heaven would that be for mice?"

She had taken such good care of Juliet, Maxine thought. It wasn't fair.

I'd have to agree.

It wasn't fair.

Death.

CHAPTER 8

The words weren't really a question so much as a statement of protest against the journalism assignment itself.

"What am I supposed to write?" Maxine asked Ben.

"Your obituary," he laughed.

"So you think it's funny, my death?"

"Of course not, but you're not dead, Max, you're very much alive and sitting at the kitchen table with a blank page in front of you, except for those bizarre sketches. How Goth of you."

Maxine peered at her work. "Never thought of myself as Goth. "

"A mini Goth, definitely. A baby bat. Part of the Goth revival. You're too young to be old school," Ben said.

"Did you call me a baby bat?"

"Yeah, I did."

"Very romantic in a Tim-Burtonesque way."

"Goth leftovers from the eighties call the kids in their black Goth get-up baby bats, mall bats and even spooky kids."

"How do you know so much about Goth?"

"*Wikipedia*," Ben said. "I've been googling here while you're procrastinating."

Maxine drew a stylized bat-hyphen after her date of birth on her obituary assignment page. "I'm not procrastinating."

"Whatever you say, Max. Okay, then, Goth history. Gothic rock is a subgenre of post-punk, and earlier than that, American punk and death rock."

Maxine ignored Ben, looked up obituaries in the index of the *Ottawa Citizen*.

Births and deaths shared the same section, the alpha and the omega.

You'd think they'd let you celebrate the beginning of life without rubbing in your face the inevitability of the end of life, Maxine thought. Give you a bit of breathing space in between...

"Then there's Goth literature," Ben continued. "Vampire books, horror genre, typical Anne Rice stuff, all of those emerging from the classic Victorian gothic novel. Want more, my little tomb creature?"

"I get the point, I'll get on with it."

Maxine spread the *Ottawa Citizen* open on the tabletop.

Scanned the page.

Except for a few variations in form, each obituary provided the same basic information: deceased's full name, year of birth, date of death.

"What do I put as my date of death?" Maxine muttered.

She scribbled some words on the page in a script she imagined to be Goth-like: *I am alive. I will die. But not today.* It was rather presumptuous on Maxine's part to assume she wouldn't die on that day. But who really thinks they are going to die on any given day, except maybe those who are imminently ill, or those who are planning suicide? Death is future tense, never present tense.

The topic of her death was one of those future-tense events Maxine hadn't spent much time pondering. In that way, she wasn't different from the other living souls she encountered on a daily basis. Maybe it wasn't her death that was really the roadblock to the assignment, but the topic of living. To write the obituary meant thinking about her life. Except for the date of one's demise, and a comment or two about how one's life ended

– *after a courageous battle with cancer* or *peacefully in her sleep with her family around her* – an obituary pretty much dealt with the facts of living.

There had been times when the events of her life had forced Maxine to think about death. Dead pets, and a dead grandfather, and a few séances, and when she was young, she had held those funeral services and burials for dead insects and small rodents. But in general, death had been a theoretical subject.

"What's in your genes?" Ben asked.

"My legs."

"DNA, Max – how long do the women usually live in your family?"

"So you're not talking about getting into my pants?"

The thought occurred to Maxine that having sex would put off writing the obituary. She looked at her watch. It was already eight o'clock, and the assignment was due the next day. They could make love, and then she could skip class tomorrow and say she had been home sick. Her journalism professor was big on detail, and his lecture echoed in her head. "Be specific. Don't simply tell readers you were home sick, tell them the nature of your illness, give it a name." She'd have to come up with an ailment, not too debilitating, just enough to keep her from class and give her a reprieve. The twenty-four-hour flu was boring, although it was contagious, and less conspicuous than a sprained ankle, which would require acting on her part. A limp and maybe props, crutches, she could check out the Goodwill the next day for a pair. But she could get a longer extension if she said there was a death in the family, probably three or four days. For the sake of detail, she'd have to assign the death to a specific family member, but who? Which of her family members to kill off? The last thought skipped briefly across her consciousness, a tumbleweed that showed itself physically as a small smile, and then disappeared.

Maxine had no suppressed desire to murder her family members. She also knew she wouldn't skip class tomorrow. She'd go, without the sprained ankle and crutches, whether the assignment was done or not, although the assignment would probably be done, in some form or another. It was her nature.

"Both my grandmothers are still alive, very healthy widows. One of my grandfathers died when I was about six. The other, I don't have any memories of him, he died on the day that my little sister, Movida, was born. All my aunts are alive on both sides of the family, although I have a few dead uncles."

"The women in your family are regular black widow spiders," Ben said. "The female black widow spiders always outlive the males. They mate and then kill their sex partners. Eat them."

"In your dreams," Maxine answered.

Maybe it was the fact that females in her bloodline did live such long healthy lives that lead Maxine to think that she would, too. It wasn't just a denial of reality or a matter of being oblivious to what was happening around her. She felt in her bones that she would grow old. It was a perspective that was bred into Maxine, resided deep down in the places of her sinew and blood cells and marrow. It was a true-north feeling, a way of situating herself that felt right. Ben, on the other hand, always said that he'd die before he was thirty. He didn't say it with fear or regret, just felt it with the same true-north feeling that Maxine felt she'd grow old. He believed he would never experience old age, unlike Maxine who equally believed she'd pass through pre-defined stages in the natural unfolding of her life. She would earn a university degree, have a career in journalism, bear a child, maybe children, get married, but if not, then certainly have a lifelong relationship with a man she loved, she would watch their children grow, participate in the everyday unfolding of their lives, their children would grow up themselves and find their own true loves, she would have grandchildren, great-grandchildren, her hair would turn snowy-white, her skin wrinkle, her eyesight and hearing dim, and someday far far down the road, she would die of old age.

"Since this is my obituary and I'm writing it, I can put any date I want for my death," Maxine thought, feeling a bit rebellious.

This was her life, after all, and her death.

She'd have her life span a perfect century; there was symmetry to that, an order, and she liked order. She would live a hundred years exactly, but then she thought better of it, didn't want to die on her birthday, would rather enjoy the celebration, the cake and ice-cream, and generations of family circling her bedside, and the many good wishes that would come her way upon reaching the centenary of her birth. So she wrote, allowing herself some first-draft embellishments that she knew would need cutting during the input-to-computer stage:

LANE, Maxine Lilli-Anne - Peacefully in her sleep, at her residence, surrounded by her loving family, on March 17, 2080. Born one hundred years and one day earlier in Brockville, Ontario, the City of the Thousand Islands, at Saint Vincent de Paul Hospital, near the banks of the mighty St. Lawrence River.

CHAPTER 9

Maxine's older sister, Adeline, fretted about the length of her lifeline, or rather the lack of it. "I'm destined to die young," she moaned on her twenty-first birthday, and still very much alive.

Maxine held her sister's palm in her own palm, studying the lines that etched Adeline's hand. "You shouldn't even have been born," she finally said.

That was true. Adeline had no lifeline. No life, either, Maxine joked when she later related the incident to Ben. Maxine's lifeline, on the hand, stretched thickly across her palm and wrapped around her wrist like a snake.

Adeline is indeed a sick woman, but not mortally sick. She just doesn't seem to be able to find any peace of mind or body. She gets headaches a lot, especially on nights of a full moon. She fully admits to her lunar sicknesses, circles the full moons on her calendar and prepares for them. She pulls the curtains shut and puts cold face cloths across her forehead and stocks up on aspirin. She doesn't eat chocolate or cheese or drink milk during these times. They give her headaches, too, a condition magnified when the gravitational pull on the ocean's tides are at their peak of power during the full moon. It's scientific, she says, and can be plotted, like astrology.

Menstruation also gives Adeline headaches. Once a month, she gets to complain about the "woman's curse." How it bloats her body and gives her cramps and affects her mind. And when her period happens to coincide with the full moon, and she has a moment of weakness and eats a chocolate bar, ("the devil made me do it"), then the full wrath of her sickness falls upon those who venture by. And after, when the full moon subsides into a slice of its former self, and the effects of the chocolate wear off, and her menstrual flow dries up, she bears no responsibility for her actions, pleading temporary insanity.

Maxine discovered this first hand. The three variables intersected - chocolate, menstruation, and a harvest moon - when Maxine visited Adeline's for a weekend break from university.

"What's that?" Adeline asked, munching on a piece of Jersey Milk chocolate bar.

"What's what?"

"Around your neck."

"Oh, that's a Buddha necklace. Movida gave it to me as a birthday gift."

Adeline's back grew rigid.

"Take it off," she said. "I'll have none of that in my house."

"I like it," Maxine responded.

At university, Maxine had been exposed to other religions, other ways of thinking. The meditating Buddha represented the concept of alternate ideas, acknowledged perspectives other than that which she had been taught at home in her Christian upbringing. When she had first worn the Buddha, Maxine thought the roof would cave in, or she'd be hit by lightning, or God would visit upon her a plague of frogs, or locusts, or grasshoppers. But no such thing had happened. Until Adeline. In hindsight, she would have preferred the plagues.

"It's a perfect night for a walk," Maxine said, looking up at the pancake moon, hoping to change the subject.

"You'll never reap the rewards of paradise," Adeline preached, refusing to be shifted from the topic at hand: Maxine's salvation.

Maxine sighed.

She could tell by Adeline's stance that her sister couldn't be swayed. Adeline had planted her feet on the ground, and held her hands on her hips.

"It's just a Buddha charm," Maxine said.

"Take it off," Adeline said.

Maxine refused. Adeline went to her bedroom, returned with a very large cross. "Here's my birthday gift. Put this on," she said.

"I don't want your gift. Keep it."

So Adeline wore the necklace, the cross dangling between her breasts, as if it could ward off evil, ward off ghosts, ward off Maxine. She harangued Maxine throughout the night. Played gospel songs on her out-dated tape recorder, and read Bible verses out loud, and argued theology, fed by the insanity of the full moon and her own blood flow. But sometimes in life there are minor victories. Victories that don't show up in history books or in the achievements listed in obituaries, and that hardly seem worthy of the telling when compared to the headlines in the newspapers, or the television news stories of the day, that pale next to the advances of science, or the latest peace talks, or other such monumental happenings.

When Adeline finally went to bed, the moon riding high and round in the night, Maxine still wore the Buddha charm about her neck.

This was her tiny victory.

✧ ✧ ✧

The first being who spoke to me in the otherworld was the Buddha.

"Is this Nirvana?" I asked.

Seemed a reasonable question to me.

The Buddha laughed. It was the kind of laugh I would

have expected from the Godhead of Zen. The heavens shook. I instinctively covered my head with my arms and crouched, thinking it must be an earthquake, or more aptly, a Nirvana-quake. But it was only his belly laugh. His belly was as vast as an ocean, as unending as the sky. He had certainly come a long way from his earthly days as Siddhartha Guatama, the Royal Highness turned anorexic holy man. Cross-legged and lotus-style, fasting under a tree until he was as skinny as a twig, death a breath away. But then a strange thing happened. Siddhartha didn't die. He got up from under that tree, legs wobbly, stomach shrunken, but mind clear. His message: Life is suffering. Avoid karma like a case of the crabs. Get off the wheel of existence. Commit cosmic suicide, so to speak. Say no to reincarnation. Shed ego like a dog sheds hair in summer. Seek Nirvana.

Here, now, in the otherworld, the Buddha paused in his laughing.

He sighed a lovely sigh. The sigh held the hint of a bell, not the start, not the middle, but the end, the point when the sound exits your decibel range.

A memory of a ring, a ghost of a ring, a sigh of a ring.

The sigh lingered.

Hung there like a smoke ring.

It felt heavenly to be out of coffin position - flat on my back, as I had been, legs pressed together, hands crossed on my chest - felt heavenly to be able to stretch. I reached my arms far above my head, swayed back and forth like a dandelion in the wind, supple and lean and long. White dandelion seeds parachuted softly around me, and from me, and through me, until I was surrounded by a white cloud of swirling particles, a small cloud of cosmic dust. When the dust settled, I sat upright in the lotus position, knotted my legs and feet comfortably in a manner Maxine could never have achieved, even if she had taken up yoga, had become a lifelong practitioner, had actually lived to be a hundred plus a day.

I took up meditation after watching the Buddha sit poker faced, as unmoved as granite, forever at a time. A fly could squat on his nose, or an elephant for that matter. He would not flinch.

Not twitch a face muscle, not blink an eye, nor wiggle a toe.
Empty the mind. Find the silence.
These were the instructions from the Enlightened One. A bunch of hokey-pokey new-age clichés, I thought, but kept my own silence. I was grateful for the company; first, the coffin being an accommodation for one, and then second, having found God, losing him again, His dissipating back into his Goth nothingness from which all things come.

I didn't want to offend the Buddha, for fear he would leave too, disappear into Nirvana or wherever it is that Enlightened Ones go. I had grown attached to the old man, a no-no in Buddhism. Attachment is downfall. Rid yourself of attachment, slough it off like a snake casts its skin, and you find peace. Or so the theory goes.

I tried various methods to empty my mind.

To find the silence, to quote a Prince.

First I became a pitcher of ice water. What could be more calming than water? But the ice cubes melted, and then evaporated upward in shimmering strips, like ghosts on the highway. So I shifted imagery. Became an empty chalkboard. But try as I might, cerebral graffiti scribbled across the blank slate of my mind. Finally I opted for the silence of the bell jar. But questions, and reasons, and mixed metaphors, and memories took voice, unrelated thoughts and images filling the vacuum.

Here is one such random thought:

It's not surprising that the victims of compassion are usually female.

True, I responded, acknowledging my own chatter, rushing to occupy the vacuum, the act creating more conversation inside my already crowded bell jar of a mind.

To tame my mind, I focused on the positioning of my body, turned my palms face up, like the whirling dervishes who reached God through spinning, head cocked gently to one side as if listening to the music of the spheres. Arms outstretched, left palm down toward the ground, connecting the dervish to the earth, right palm up toward the sky, connecting the dervish to the heavens. Since I was dead and already disconnected from the earthly, I turned both palms up, as if that action might bring me understanding. Serve as conduit for the energies of the cosmos to channel through my fingertips. Light me up like a light bulb. I wanted to be a Buddha struck by enlightenment. Instant understanding, like mashed potatoes from a box. Add milk, stir, heat, and voila! I understand. Life and death.

"I yearn for paradise," I whispered, breathing the words in, breathing the words out. The Buddha broke his silence, opened his mouth and spilled out thunder, and earthquake, and tornado, and tsunami, spilled out fire and lightning.

"Nirvana isn't all it's cracked up to be," he roared, and I realized that the sound gushing headlong from the pit of his belly was his own laughter.

There's a lot more laughter on the other side than Maxine would have expected, could have imagined, being a writer and all.

CHAPTER 10

The creep had followed her.
Followed her.
"He likes you," Golda said.
"*Likes* me?"
"That's how boys show it when they're ten years old."
What was her mother talking about, saying he *liked* her?
"And what if he didn't like me? What would he do then?" Maxine asked angrily.

She didn't understand. He had been so mean to her - what did cruelty have to do with liking someone? Maxine had barely escaped on her bike down a side alley. The boy darted down another on his bike. She rode one street. He rode the parallel street, setting his pace by her, arriving at the street corner at the exact same time she did, even though he couldn't possibly have seen her through the houses, the back yards, the front lawns that had separated them. He timed it so they both reached the stop sign at the same time, but a street apart.

How did he do it?

She picked up speed, sprinted for a block, then slowed down, soft-pedalled. And still he kept pace with her, until finally, unexpectedly, he changed course, veered down a side street, cut her off.

Maxi dismounted, stood spread-eagle so that the bike was between her legs. She gripped the handlebars. "I hate you," she said, in a rare show of defiance.

The boy's face melted, as if he might cry.

Then his expression hardened.

He looked wildly at the ground, searching for a rock to throw. He put down his bike, bent over, picked something up, pounced at Maxi before she could react. Grabbed her collar, pulled it opened, dropped a dead sparrow down her shirt.

Maxi could not believe he had done this to her.

She crazily danced on her toes, shook her shirt from her body so that the dead sparrow fell at her feet. Then with strength she didn't know she had, with anger she didn't know she possessed, Maxi stepped over the crossbar, lifted up her bicycle and tossed it at the boy.

✧ ✧ ✧

There were other wars. Each winter, the route to and from school became a war zone. The war lasted the duration of the season, beginning with the first storm that left enough snow on the ground to pack balls, and re-occurred like ritual every year until Maxine graduated to high school and the boys chased the girls in more subtle ways.

During the war years, Maxine plotted strategy - which path to take to avoid the boys, which path to take to outsmart them - changing pace randomly to avoid patterns. At the sounding of the dismissal bell, she'd pull on her coat and boots, and race ahead home before the boys left the schoolyard. Sometimes instead she'd dawdle, organize her pencils, straighten her desk, volunteer for a chore, clean the blackboards, shelve library books in order using the Dewey Decimal System with all of its delicious intricacies. It didn't occur to Maxi to wonder why the girls were the victims and the boys the aggressors, why she and her girlfriends didn't organize, hide behind trees and bushes and snow outcrops, shape snowballs in the cups of their hands, and hurl the snowballs at the boys with the same tenacity and anger that she had thrown her bike.

On this winter day, Maxi instinctively ducked at the first sight of the boys, lifted her arm to protect her face. A snowball landed on an icy patch just beyond her, skidded, and then stopped atop a ridge of glistening snow. Then another. "Dead-on," a boy yelled, the tassels of a toque jumping up and down. Ice coated the trees, and the boys now put ice chunks into the centre of the snowballs. The sidewalks were sheets of ice, making escape difficult, but if she made it to Pearl Street, she could duck into the corner store. The boys might follow her, wait outside, but she would outwait them, and they'd grow bored and go home. Maxi ran, slipped on the ice, ran some more, slipped some more, then finally pushed through the door of the store. She leaned against the glass to catch her breath, loosened her scarf and hat. Wandered the aisles. Dug into her pocket for a quarter and bought a gumball. Sucked on it, the gumball bulging from her cheek, deforming her face.

Maxi peeked out of the store. The street appeared clear. She dashed outside, wildly slipping on the sidewalk, losing her footing. She fell, smashed her elbow with such a force that she thought surely her bone protruded up and through her skin. She clutched her arm tightly, half-walked, half-ran the distance home, her strange gait caused by the stiffening of one side of her body, shoulder hunched, the other shoulder drooped. Dragged herself past the hospital, even though somewhere in her muddled awareness she knew she would surely end up there, dragged herself past the high school that she would attend the next year, dragged herself through the park, and home.

George's work boots sat in the hallway like soldiers at attention. They were the only boots on the mat, which meant Golda was not home. Maxi heard George puttering in the kitchen. She did not call for him, went straight into the bathroom, shut the door, leaned against it. She grew faint, her skin clammy, her consciousness narrowing. Still she did not call out for her father.

Why, she couldn't really say, except she thought he might be angry with her for slipping on the ice. She knew the thought was unreasonable, but she thought it anyway. Her focus narrowed, until there was only a tunnel of light. Her knees buckled, so that she slid with her back against the door to the linoleum.

"Maxi?"

George spoke gently, hesitantly.

Maxi had never before heard him talk that way, so unsure of himself, as if afraid to hear the answer to the question, all possibilities of every bad happening pushed up into his conscious mind from where it resided in his place of fears.

Maxi slid her body from the door so that George could enter the room. He looked at her and she saw her pain in his eyes. She thought he might cry. She had never seen him cry, but then, she didn't remember her own funeral.

✧ ✧ ✧

George couldn't protect Maxine from hurt in all its many forms, although I don't think he ever fully accepted the fact. Fathers and daughters. The need to protect is inherent in the relationship, if not between all daughters and fathers, then between Maxine and George. He felt the need to protect her against falls and broken bones, snowballs and tire irons, against men who would hurt her, steal her virginity, steal her self-worth, lead her down the garden path. Bogeymen who'd wait in dark corners, the paedophile, the stalker, the kidnapper, the murderer, the man-next-door secretly watching her within the dark roads of his mind.

Golda knew she couldn't fully protect Maxine, not in the end, when all things were said and done. Perhaps it is a gender thing, this knowledge that you cannot truly protect another, an understanding that comes from childbirth. Birthing is a solitary act; a woman cannot be protected from the pain of labour, even by her own mother.

But that fact didn't stop Golda from trying to protect

Maxine.

Golda insisted that Maxine put in the landline phone in the small studio apartment she rented in the basement of an old house in the Glebe area of Ottawa her second year at university. "Why bother?" Maxine asked. "It's just extra money I can't afford, and I always have my cell with me."

"I'll pay the bill for the phone," Golda told her. "What if I need to get hold of you, and your cell battery is dead, or you've turned it off, or you see it is your mother phoning and refuse to answer?"

"You can always text me."

"Don't be a smart-ass."

Golda knew that Maxine knew it would take her an hour to text out a simple message. Her fingers and thumb didn't think that way, in the Morse-code, dot-to-dot action of text messaging. "What if there's an emergency and you need to talk to your father and me, and you can't find your cell phone under the pillows and clothes and empty pizza boxes strewn all over the place?"

"Then I'll borrow a cell. Use it to locate mine. Then phone you."

"So people will be at your place at all hours of the day and night to lend you a cell phone if you need it?"

Golda was, granted, worried about Maxine's safety, living alone in the city core, all the dangerous things that could happen to her, coming from a small town, although granted, Ottawa wasn't exactly the crime capital of the world. But danger in Golda's mind didn't only mean drug dealers and rapists and murderers and thieves. There were other kinds of danger.

Golda never came out in a straightforward way and asked Maxine if she and Ben were having sex, which is what she really meant when she referred to "people," generic plural, instead of Ben, masculine singular, being at the house at all times of the day and night. Golda wanted to protect her daughter from sex, yes, but also from associated conditions, such as pregnancy, a bun in the oven, her way of putting it. She focused her efforts on Maxine, Adeline being too much of a prude to possibly get pregnant, and Movida too street-smart to get herself knocked up.

Three sisters raised under a single roof, same parents, same upbringing, yet each sibling dramatically different. Oldest sister Adeline, in her later years, developed a rare disability the doctor called conversion hysteria. Probably to this day she still blacks out when she hears sex-related language. She cannot hear words like orgasm, or oral sex, or erection, or ejaculation, or masturbation, or penis (although peter-thing is obviously okay) without fainting dead to the world. Dead as Maxine in her coffin, to see Adeline lying there, on the ground, eyes closed, body limp, face chalk-white, although she always did manage to crumple on a soft surface, the long grass, or the couch, or a plush rug.

Little sister Movida energetically flaunted sex. Golda hated rings anywhere but on fingers, so Movida pierced her nose and her right nipple. George disapproved of interracial marriages, so Movida dated an African-Canadian. Both parents abhorred open displays of affection, so Movida kissed her boyfriend in public, opened her mouth and swallowed his tongue, let him put his hand up the back of her blouse, finger her bra clip, all this sex-play in broad daylight.

Middle-born among the sisters, guided by that unlikely blend of action and reticence, Maxine took the middle ground. She didn't faint, but neither did she turn a deaf ear to Golda's hang-ups and fears. Her early little-girl knowledge of sex was riddled with misconceptions extrapolated from her mother's aphorisms and warnings. "Keep your feet planted firmly on the floor," Golda warned her daughters when they left the house, each in her own stage of puberty. "And don't drink from someone else's glass." Young Maxine thought pregnancy could be caught like a cold, that she could become pregnant by sharing a coke, using a public toilet, or kissing. After the first of Becky's boy-girl parties, she tortured herself for having kissed a boy on the couch, the soles of her shoes breaking contact with the ground - tortured herself with the thought of a bun in her oven.

When Maxine went to university, Golda phoned the landline at odd times to see who answered the phone, or if anyone answered at all, meaning Maxine had stayed overnight at Ben's house and all that implied.

"Called at six this morning," Golda said, when she phoned later that same evening, a few minutes before midnight to be exact. "Nobody answered."

"Was that you?" Maxine yawned, pretending that Golda had woken her up. "I was dead tired, ignored the ring."

"Why did you do that?" Golda was suspicious but now also equally perturbed by the admission of an ignored ring. "What if someone had passed away, your father or even me, and we needed to tell you?"

"If it were you who had passed away, you wouldn't be telephoning me, would you?" Maxine said.

She lifted her finger to her lips, motioning Ben to be quiet.

Ben rolled down to the bottom of the bed, dressed in his boxers. He sucked her toes, licked the bottom of her feet to make her giggle.

"What's so funny?" Golda asked. "My passing?"

"Not at all," Maxine said, more giggling, Ben moving up her leg to her thigh.

At least, Golda's passing was no funnier than any other.

CHAPTER 11

Four children, three girls and one boy, all in the same family, none of whom was adopted, none of whom was conceived under supernatural circumstances, such as visitation by God, or alien abduction, as far as I know. Neither were they cloned, or mixed in a test-tube, or made through other methods of scientifically engineered genetics. So it stands to reason sex must have occurred in Maxine's family sphere at least four times. It is a mystery that ranks right up there with creation itself: one would think sex, or at least things of a sexual nature, was something that couldn't be hidden in such a big brood living under a single roof, that the children would have awakened on occasion to the rhythmic pounding of the headboard, or an orgasmic cry, or a wheedling plea of desire. The odds were also good over the span of their childhood, that Peter and the sisters would bump into each other in various stages of nudity, running away in shock, perhaps, but not before taking a good hard look at what the other had or didn't have. But it never happened, at least not to Maxine, not that she remembered, or I remembered.

Adeline did claim that Peter once brushed up against her as they passed in opposite directions down the narrow hallway; she in her nightgown, his "peter-thing" hard and stiff under his pajama bottoms. She made this revelation to Maxine ten years later. They sat together on the front porch on the hot sticky summer night and wondered aloud what had happened to all the fireflies. "Peter brushed his peter-thing against me," Adeline said, handling with relative ease the unlikely transition in conversation from fireflies to peter-things, considering her array of hang-ups and emotional ailments and physical conditions. "I was twelve years old and he was fifteen. I thought he had a banana in his trousers."

Maxine did not know if the brushing incident were real; and if real, intentional; or if it existed only within her sister's head; or if Peter actually did stick a banana down his pants. Human existence is like that, lacking absolutes. What one person perceives as truth has no guarantee outside that person.

Maybe that's the attraction to life, this lack of absolutes.

Random chances and insanities, personal perceptions and opportunities, tangled to form a single lifetime, a knot of sensations, and delights, and horrors, and manias that belong to one person alone. I thought about that a lot, too, in the otherworld, sitting twisted like a pretzel in lotus position.

✧ ✧ ✧

Golda wasn't the only person who told Maxine that a boy liked her.

"Go on, behind the bushes," Peter whispered into Maxi's ear. "He's waiting, he likes you."

The little girl stood hesitantly in the yard behind their house. She looked at her big brother, looked away and toward the window of her house. The curtains were closed. Golda was busy, probably ironing or doing laundry. She turned toward Peter again.

"What's the matter, chicken?" Peter pushed, his voice harder.

Maxi felt hurt by the change in tone. She had enjoyed

this camaraderie with her brother, this conspiratorial intimacy. They usually fought, or he teased her, Maxi inevitably bursting into tears, *Mommy, Mommy, Peter's being mean to me.* But this was different, this new relationship between them. She didn't want it to end. She smiled at Peter. He smiled back. She liked being liked by him. So Maxi skipped to the bush, ankle socks, shiny black patent leather shoes, pretty skirt of the blue dress Golda had made flouncing around her legs. Peter hadn't lied. The boy waited behind the bushes. She looked at him expectantly, and then he did it. He kissed her.

Maxi ran smiling from the bushes, ran smiling to Peter.

"Boy, oh boy. Will Mama ever be mad at you," he said.

Maxi felt confused.

What did he mean? Golda would be mad?

But Peter should know, he was older than her, and he should know.

"Mama's gonna beat you silly," he said. "You, back behind a bush neckin' with a boy. Boy oh boy, you're gonna get it now."

Golda had never before beaten Maxi silly.

What had she done so terrible that Golda would start now?

She had let the boy kiss her, that's what. She had gone behind the bushes. Hadn't been dragged there kicking and screaming. Hadn't been forced. She was guilty. She felt her face flush hot with shame.

"Don't tell her," Maxi said. "Please don't tell her."

"Maybe I will and maybe I won't," Peter said.

For a long while, Maxi stayed out of Peter's way, especially around Golda. The little girl paid close attention to the conversation, pretending not to pay attention, dressing and undressing her doll, colouring a picture, steering the conversation away from bushes, or kissing, or anything else that could be remotely connected, that could prompt the telling, *guess what Maxi did, that naughty girl?*

Maxi kept the memory of her shame deep inside.

When she was older, Maxine realized that she had

done nothing wrong, that the behind-the-bush incident hadn't warranted the shame she had felt. But you can't easily erase a shame, rub it out like a pencil mark on a piece of paper.
    It marks you for life.
    And for death, it seems, too.
    Indelible shames as deep and dark as a little girl's fantasies.

✧ ✧ ✧

The hollyhocks at the side of the house weren't yet in bloom, flowers still unborn, hard thick green buds, but Maxi remembered the glorious riot of flowers from last year, the first summer that she could truly remember, without everything and everybody sliding into each other. If she were patient, the hollyhocks would return, she fantasized, just as Golda had promised. The hollyhocks stretched taller than Maxi, and the stems were thick. They looked as if they could not be broken, would fight being snapped in half and put in a vase like the other flowers, only to be thrown out later when they were dead and people were tired of them.
    She compared the pale pink flowers of the hollyhocks to the bright petunias and marigolds that George planted in the flower boxes and along the edges of the yard. Maxi liked the hollyhocks better than George's flowers, because they didn't have to be planted every year, just grew on their own. She imagined how nice it would be to live in a tiny house painted the pale pink of hollyhocks with lacy curtains the same pale pink, and how, if she lived in such a tiny house, all by herself, she'd keep the window open so that the wind fluttered the ruffles on the pale pink curtains, and she could watch the pale pink hollyhocks grow next to her pale pink cottage, fields of hollyhocks as far as she could see.
    This was Maxi's first childhood fantasy.
    Maxi's second childhood fantasy occurred when

Golda took her to watch Adeline dance around the Maypole, the Maypole really the school flagpole decorated with bright streamers. Maxi fantasized that she were older, didn't have to sit in a stroller, longed for it, to grow up and go to school and dance around the Maypole with her classmates, too. She imagined it, her hair fluttering behind her in the breeze like ruffles of a curtain in an open window. Maxi skipped around the flagpole, the ribbon wound about her hand, palms closed tightly so she wouldn't drop the end, wouldn't break the circle. Her footsteps inscribed intricate patterns, never missing a step, never stumbling, weaving her way through the other dancers, under their ribbons, under their arms. Bright ribbons stretched from the top of the flagpole to the children like spokes of a giant wheel. Around and around they danced, planets to the sun, the moon to the earth, part of a greater good, and if not a good, then a part of something greater, her world revolving happily in some kind of wonderful carousel.

  Her third childhood fantasy embarrassed Maxine when she grew old enough to feel embarrassment, even shame. Why would a child think such things?

  She'd push the memory away and refuse to think about it, but it was another one of those marks you can't rub out. The fantasy arose with school. Kindergarten and the fantasy joined in her mind like two schoolgirls holding hands. It began with Aylmer Cox, a box-shaped boy who talked incessantly. Talked in class without putting up his hand first, talked without asking permission, talked without hesitation, talked unabashedly about everything and anything that entered his mind - the birds at the window, his father's peg leg, his mother's girdle. As soon as words popped into Aylmer's head, they popped out of his mouth.

  Maxi waited in line at the school door of her kindergarten class, as she was supposed to wait, until the bell rang. She walked indoors single file, didn't run or push, put her rolled-up blanket in the cubby hole that bore her name, put her snack in the cubby hole, too. Hung up her sweater on her hook, put up her hand to speak, asked permission, spoke politely, worked hard at her painting, sang the songs with enthusiasm but didn't drown out the other children, never fought in the schoolyard, and when the time came, spread her blanket on the floor, ate her snack, closed her eyes and napped.

Golda called Miss Finstra, the kindergarten teacher, a spinster.

Maxi imagined her teacher going home each night and spinning in her room like a top. Miss Finstra was a thin, tired-faced woman with jet-black hair without a strand of grey, although she had lived an eternity, maybe longer, long enough that the alphabet cut-outs strung on the wall over the chalkboard had faded, long enough that she had developed a school routine for everything, from asking to go to the washroom (put up your hand, hold up two fingers, and wait patiently – do not bounce up and down or hold yourself *you-know-where*) to singing the Good Morning Song first thing everyday. Lived long enough to collect an infinity of empty aluminium juice cans to rinse paintbrushes, long enough to have a myriad of rules, important rules that must be followed, otherwise there would be *chaos in the world* and the children were the *adults of the future*.

Miss Finstra taught the children songs and rhymes. She taught them this one: *Aylmer Cox is a chatterbox*. She encouraged them to sing the verse often, in the schoolyard before school started, screeching the verse when Aylmer came into view, pointing at him and laughing, in the classroom whispering the verse quietly so not to disturb Grade One down the hall. But still Aylmer talked, so Miss Finstra sat Aylmer on the stool so that he stared out the big picture window that faced the street, his back to the rest of the children. She made Aylmer stick out his tongue and then she clipped the clothespin to the end of it. "There," she announced. "Now the whole world will know that Aylmer Cox is a naughty chatterbox."

Aylmer sat on the stool, all morning, unable to say a word, a clothespin stuck to the end of his tongue. Maxi felt horrified for him. She thought she might cry, although she didn't, accepted the fact that somehow he deserved this punishment if Miss Finstra had meted it out. But at night, when she was alone in bed in the dark, with only her little-girl thoughts, she fantasized she sat facing out the window, the clothespin on her tongue, punishment for being a naughty girl. Sometimes there were other punishments, spankings administered by a person of great authority, a person of great wisdom, who understood such things, knew right and wrong in an ultimate sense, and rendered judgment.

  This was her third fantasy.
  A patriarchal God.

CHAPTER 12

No big deal, Maxine told herself, pushing away the guilt of self-punishment. We were just kids. It's not as if I did something really terrible, like tossed a cat in the river. I didn't do anything. Why should I feel shame?

But she felt shame anyway. It was the "not-doing" that marked her.

"I'm your cousin," the new kid at school said to Maxi. "Your third cousin. Do you want me to show you the family tree?"

Maxi didn't want to know how she could be related to the new girl, didn't want the new girl spreading the word about the school that they were *cousins*. But Maxi also felt sorry for the new girl, couldn't help it. Once, she even went to Peg's house. Peg's mother insisted that Maxi call her Auntie. She made them a chocolate cake and smothered it with chocolate icing. The items in the house were worn and poor, second-hand looking, third- or fourth-hand, really. Golda shopped at the discount stores, traded clothes with friends, and went to a church rummage sale every third Tuesday of the month, but the things she brought home didn't look the same as the things in Peg's house, didn't look like the used clothes Peg wore. And Peg was so eager. She hung around Maxine like a puppy dog, wanted so badly to be one of the gang.

"It's pitiful," Becky said one day after school. "Is she really your cousin?"

Maxine didn't answer, but Golda had confirmed the tenuous bloodline. Somebody Maxine didn't even know marrying somebody she couldn't care less about giving birth to somebody who happened to be Peg's mother.

Who put the red paint on Peg's chair, no one could say for sure.

No one admitted to it later when the principal spoke to the class.

But there it was, when Peg sat down, and then stood up, red paint smeared like blood across her skirt, the class laughing and pointing at her, someone yelling, "Peg's got her period."

Peg just stood there, red paint across her skirt, on her hand too from touching the chair. Then touching her face, red paint on her cheek.

She just stood there. Waiting for Maxine to intervene.

Looking to Maxine. And waiting.

✧ ✧ ✧

Like a voyeur, Maxi watched Becky and Joel cling to each other. She wondered if her best friend was nervous slow dancing with Joel, their chests touching like that, if her palms sweated, or her underarms. Becky's father leaned against the archway, and she expected him to yell at them, for turning out the lights at Becky's boy-girl party, for dancing in the dark, for dancing at all. George would have screamed bloody murder. But Becky's father didn't yell, just took a swig of beer, held the bottle straight up to drain it.

"Got a game to show you," he said.

He arranged them into a circle, boy-girl-boy-girl-boy-girl-boy-girl.

Then he knelt in the centre and spun the empty beer bottle on the floor.

The bottleneck pointed to Becky.

"Kiss me," her father said, making a joke of puckering.

Becky laughed, and kissed him on the lips, a good long smack.

"Now it's your turn," he told her.

Becky spun the bottle and the neck pointed at Joel. They kissed, held it so long that everyone hooted, and Becky's dad hooted with them. Joel spun, kissed Maxi - her first kiss – nothing Cinderella about it. Maxi spun the bottle, kissed Shawn, a quick peck, and so it went throughout the evening.

Maxi stayed behind to clean up the mess, too excited to go home yet, head and heart spinning with the dizziness of kisses and slow dances in the dark.

"Sleepover?" Becky asked.

"Sure," Maxi said. "But shouldn't you check with your dad?"

Becky picked up the empty beer bottle off the floor and stashed it in the last empty space in the return carton. "He's passed out, dead to the world, and Mom's working a double shift. Anyway, they'd say yes."

The two girls talked into the night, rating kisses and rating boys, until Maxi fell asleep in Becky's bed, and Becky curled up in the rollaway cot in the corner. Maxi woke up in the dark, in that sudden way, where you surface from a deep sleep, and don't know where you are. Rather, she was woken up, that passive tense again. She smelled his presence at the same time she felt it. George didn't drink, so the smell of beer was stale and sickening to her, made her want to throw up. Becky's father loomed over her, his hand under her nightgown, cupping her small breasts.

"It's me, Maxine," Maxi said.

Becky's father mumbled something Maxi couldn't later remember and hurried from the room. Maxi pondered what had happened, kept the happening to herself, didn't know what to call it, or how to define it. Didn't know the right words. Didn't know what to say so didn't say anything. Didn't speak to Becky about it, didn't ask her if she had been molested as a child, even when they were older and knew the words. It's another act of "not-doing" that marked her, and if it didn't mark her, that I have come to regret.

✦ ✦ ✦

I can't detach from the memory of her life, can't detach from *Maxine*.

We're attached, like a lifeline between mother ship and floating astronaut.

Then how can I expect enlightenment?

Attachment is the Buddhist equivalent to a cardinal sin. No light bulbs flashing on in my head, no instant answers served like mashed potatoes on a plate. At least, no answers to the traditional questions one might be expected to ask at the end of life. Why was Maxine born? Why did she die? What is the otherworld? Is her death karma? Is there a God? Does it matter?

But maybe it's not enlightenment I'm seeking. Maybe it's redemption. Forgiveness of sins. Fire and brimstone, judgment rendered and served. But what sins, really? Maxine might have been guilty of some minor wrongdoing, but no capital offences, nothing to warrant the death penalty, death by tire iron at the side of the road. God Almighty in heaven, I think not!

"You're guilty as sin."

The voice and words startled me out of lotus-position.

I looked for the body that had spit forth the voice, but this was the otherworld. Voices do not need bodies. The voice continued with the smugness of revelation itself. "Light bulbs and instant potatoes, karma and whirling dervishes. Guilty as charged! Guilty of mixing metaphors. No good journalist would mix metaphors! Case closed."

The magnified bang of a gavel rocked me, and the heavens spilled open with thunder and lightning and all the theatrics of judgment. Then the voice softened, and sunshine spilled out from behind the deep black clouds – the proverbial ray of hope. "It's really no big deal in a cosmic sense, all sins considered, just thought you'd want it pointed out, having been trained as a journalist."

"Who said anything about whirling dervishes?" I said nastily, pissed off that I had been caught mixing metaphors by a disembodied voice. "And anyway, who died and put you in charge?"

"Have faith, you *will* say something about whirling dervishes."

The voice spoke with unhurried confidence, a rich tenor with a comforting quality, like old fine wood polished with lemon oil, so that I immediately felt soothed. It struck me with the force of enlightenment that maybe the voice *was* in charge, *The Voice.*

I stammered an apology, but Nobody was listening.

The Voice had slipped back into the Silence whence It came.

"Did you hear that?" I asked the Buddha incredulously.

But he ignored me, just sat there, undisturbed, had meditated right through the entire Voice encounter. I attempted to return to my own meditation, but I was unable to concentrate on nothingness, kept listening for the Voice. So I gave up, opened my eyes. It's a good thing. A dot appeared in the distance, gathered shape and size, acting most unlike a dot, kicking up dust and charging towards me until a collision was inevitable. But this is the otherworld. Nothing is inevitable.

The dot turned into an elephant and careened to a sudden stop, raised its trunk, let loose a mighty trumpet, loud enough and mighty enough to tumble the Walls of Jericho if this were ancient Judea, to set off an earthquake and set forth a tsunami if this were the South Pacific. I ran in terror for a hiding place, abandoned the Buddha, searched vainly for high land or the forest, but the landscape stretched prairie-flat, as flat as the landscape of my father's prairie youth. So I stood out there in open space, unprotected, nothing to hide behind, not even my words. The elephant reared up, towered over the Buddha so that everything grew dark, like an eclipse had cast a shadow on the earth, and then the elephant lowered its legs, lowered its body, squarely on top of the Enlightened One.

I thought the weight would surely crush the Buddha.

I awaited his fate.

And waited.

And waited.

Eventually, the elephant grew bored.

Lifted itself off the Buddha, and ambled off into the distance, the ground swaying, the earthquakes, or more exactly, the otherworld-quakes settling into small ripples, until the elephant was a dot in the distance again. The Buddha sat intact, un-squashed, not a dent or mark on him. I poked him in the belly and waited for a sign of life. His stone face sank into a slow smile that spread across the expanse of nothingness. "You're not dead!" I exclaimed with a mixture of relief and amazement.

"On the contrary. I'm very dead," he said. "So how can an elephant *kill* me?"

There's a certain freedom in knowing you're dead and nothing can kill you.

"Hu," the Buddha trumpeted, emitting a noise not unlike the elephant, expelling a rush of air that sent me tumbling head over heels, head over heels, head over heels through the vast open expanse of the otherworld.

To borrow from Newton: A body in motion tends to stay in motion unless acted upon by an outside force. Take Maxine, for example. She was certainly in motion until that man with the car on the side of the road acted upon her. Put her out of motion. Stopped her dead in her tracks.

My head hurt from the incessant tumbling.

Still I tumbled, kilometre upon kilometre, decade upon decade, until distance and time had no more relevance, until I no longer felt dizzy with my rolling, but felt strangely contented by it. Rolled with the rolling, so to speak. Flowed with the flow, to give it a Taoist spin. But all things do come to an end. I came to rest, acted upon abruptly by an outside force. I crashed headlong into the Buddha's belly, had come full circle, my starting point now my end point.

The Buddha was meditating.

What's new?

Nothing, it seems. Here he was, calm and eternally unmoved, while I had been rolling head-over-heels through endless space and time. He could have at least pretended to miss me, to have noticed I was gone, after all that rolling, after all the death.

The Enlightened One began to spin.

I grew aware of my own spinning motion that had always been, that I hadn't noticed before, like Earthlings do not feel the revolutions of the planet. I opened my hand and saw solar systems held within it, planets spinning against blackness around suns. The Buddha rolled himself into a ball and closed his eyes. I rolled myself up too, like a baby in a womb, knees drawn toward my chest, arms pressed close. I orbited Buddha like the moon around the Earth, while Buddha turned around a larger Buddha. And so on. And so on. Inscribing the pattern of the solar system, turning on our own axis, too. Planets and solar systems like whirling dervishes.

"Told you!" the Voice said.

Whirling dervishes.

I closed my eyes and spun, and in the spinning forgot myself.

Forgot Buddha, and Maxine, and the Voice.

Forgot all.

There was peace in forgetting.

Peace in darkness.

All the lights turned out.

CHAPTER 13

Maxine felt awkward around machines. Well, most machines. There were exceptions. Maxine came to feel quite at home with her laptop computer, manoeuvred around the word processing program like a racing car driver at the steering wheel. It was the under-the-console details she couldn't handle, the under-the-hood kind of things, the inner workings. When she got her driver's license, and the windshield fluid ran out of her car, she drove to a service station to have it refilled rather than opening the hood, and unscrewing the top to the jug and pouring the fluid in all by herself. So it is completely understandable that when she saw a car at the side of the road, hood raised in the universal sign of distress, she didn't suspect a ruse. Didn't doubt for one moment that the machinery under that hood had broken down in the middle of the night on such a godforsaken and lonely stretch of highway. Didn't doubt that machines were as much a mystery to this poor soul as to herself, stranding the unfortunate sot to an unknown fate, at very least, a sad cold night at the side of the road. Didn't occur to her that the only poor sot at the side of the road would turn out to be herself.

Some people are born with an innate understanding

of the mechanical. Take apart an antique Swiss clock with all those delicate springs and sprockets, mix up the parts, and they easily put it back together. The headlight on the car goes out and they buy a bulb and replace it; the fan belt needs replacing, no problem. Maxine was not one of those people. She lacked the mechanical gene in her DNA necklace. She didn't understand the workings of sprockets and pulleys and switches and pistons. She didn't know the basic tools of machinery and construction. She couldn't identify a screw from a nut from a bolt. Recognized a screwdriver, but didn't know the different kinds: Phillips, Square, Star, Flat. Recognized a nail, but didn't know the relevance of sizes or types. Couldn't repair basic items around the house such as a drippy faucet or a creaky door. Couldn't locate the circuit box or the water shut-off valve. She could, however, change a light bulb, although she never shook the nagging fear, whenever she unscrewed the old bulb from the socket or screwed the new bulb in place, that she'd electrocute herself.

In Junior High, the teachers implemented standardized testing to measure abilities in several scholastic areas: reading, writing, mathematics, logic, and mechanical reasoning. Maxine scored in the top five percent of students across the province in her age group in the literacy categories. She scored in the top fifteen percent for logic (the testing involved primarily language and number sequencing problems), and fell squarely in the middle of the pack for mathematics - half of those tested scored higher than Maxine, and half lower. In the mechanical reasoning portion, Maxine scored in the bottom five percentile. She was mechanically challenged, maybe even a mechanical imbecile. For the life of her, she couldn't decipher the line drawings of pulleys and other strange items; if one sprocket turned this way, what way did the other sprocket turn? Maxine was bewildered.

Perhaps Maxine had inherited an extra wallop of George-genes.

Whenever Maxine's father, George, put together a boxed shelving unit or bookcase or desk using the packaged instructions, the task took him all afternoon and several attempts, and there were pieces left over. If he built something from scratch, even with the use of a level, the finished item would be crooked or have a gap where there shouldn't be a gap. The breakfast nook he built for the kitchen pinched Maxine's bum if she sat on the bench where the lumber didn't line up, and the matching flowerboxes he built for the front porch didn't match, one several centimetres longer than the other. The pictures George put on the wall always hung a bit crooked. Cockeyed, Golda called them, tilting her head to one side. Since George had trouble with basic handyman tasks, he assumed that his children had the same trouble. He wouldn't let them touch the tools, or take apart discarded household items to find out how they worked, wouldn't let them fix common household breakdowns like leaky faucets, or replace blown fuses.

Maxine's friend, Becky, scored a rating of genius on the mechanical reasoning test. She was a mechanical Einstein. That, too, was part nature, part nurture. Becky's dad got called by the school whenever there was a problem the janitor couldn't fix, such as a boiler boiling over, or the Canadian flag tangled around the top of the flagpole.

"Hey, look," Aylmer Cox shouted in the middle of the morning announcements one day, pointing out the third-story window of the grade six class room. There, parallel to their line of vision, was Becky's dad, legs wrapped around the uppermost part of the flagpole. He pulled tools out of his tool belt easily, as if he sat on the ground and not ten metres up. Replaced the rusted screws, squirted the pulley with grease, untangled the flag so that it blew unfettered, then slid down the pole with the sleekness of a fire fighter.

On Saturday mornings, Becky bought the week's groceries for her family.

The responsibility amazed Maxine. She never got to buy the family's groceries, or help her father change the tread-worn tires of the car, or hammer nails into lumber to build a patio, or switch the propane barbecue tank and then light the barbecue for burgers. Becky used the automated checkout to pay for the groceries, pulled the family debit card out of her jacket pocket, another fact that caused Maxine to marvel. At twelve years of age, she had never been entrusted with the family debit card, let alone been told the PIN so she could pay for a purchase.

To use the debit card meant using a machine. George had nightmares, actual nightmares, that the ATM would chew up the card, or embezzle money from him by adding a zero to his withdrawal, his savings disappearing into a cyber hellhole. If the machine might do that kind of harm to him, what might it do to Maxine?

When Maxine stayed over at Becky's house the night of the boy-girl party, she helped Becky buy the groceries the next morning. Maxine thought it a great adventure, pushing the cart down the aisles, finding the items on the grocery list. Becky thought Maxine was certifiably crazy. Becky would rather be home watching DVDs or playing video games. She said she wished her dad were more like George, but she didn't elaborate, and Maxine didn't ask.

The coffee grinder at the grocery store amazed Maxine. First, her parents drank instant coffee. Second, the coffee grinder was a machine put in the public space of the grocery store for anyone to use, even her. "You get the coffee – fine grind, dark roast, Columbian," Becky said to Maxine, reading from the list, and then disappearing down the toilet paper aisle. Maxine waited for Becky to reappear, but she didn't. So Maxine read the instructions carefully, then re-read them, and re-read them again, hesitantly followed them, fully expecting the machine to break, or refuse to work for her.

Miraculously, the grinder spit out coffee as per the instructions, although Maxine pulled the bag too soon from under the spout, sending a spray of fine grinds to the floor, but in the grand scale of life, what are a few grinds on the floor, when the machine actually worked?

✧ ✧ ✧

"Be careful," George warned Maxi when she went on an escalator. "You could lose a leg if your pant hem gets caught."

Little Maxi heeded her father's advice, froze deathly still while riding the escalator, didn't move, except to breathe, and maybe not even then, holding her breath inside of her as if she were underwater. All of the stairs she had encountered up to this point in her seven years of life had stayed still.

She jumped off the end of the escalator a step or two before it was level with the floor, in case her pant hem got caught or the hem of her coat, or perhaps nothing at all, the escalator simply choosing to swallow her. The escalator, after all, was a machine. Although artificial intelligence was still sci-fi, she didn't doubt for a second that it just might make a purposeful, albeit malevolent decision, to chew her up and spit her out in little pieces, a coffee grinder gone mad.

An elevator is not an escalator, granted, but to Maxine's way of thinking, they were first cousins. And deep-seated fears are hard to shake, if for no other reason than they are deep-seated.

The Arts Tower, the tallest building at Carleton University, contained an elevator. Maxine's fourth-year university class, "Ethics and the Journalist," took place on the eighteenth floor. If she were early for class, Maxine took the stairs, huffing and puffing long before she reached the top, convincing herself that fitness was the reason she avoided the elevator. If she had nothing important after class, she'd take the stairs down too, a much easier process, but still time-consuming.

Most of the time, Maxine was late for her class and took the elevator by evil necessity. She told herself her fears were irrational, that more people died in car crashes, even airplane crashes, than elevator crashes. But the study of statistics and probabilities did little to allay her fears. The journalist's nature such as it is, she searched out the peculiar and obscure, the exception to the rule. To find it, all she had to do was read the newspaper, which she did daily. A woman killed by a runaway tire, wheeling over her lawn, missing an apple tree, crashing through a bay window, rolling down a hallway, hitting her from behind and breaking her neck as she drank coffee in the sanctity of her own home. A teenager killed when a hunk of frozen waste fell from an airplane and tumbled through his roof hitting him two-stories below while he slept on a couch in the recreation room of his basement after coming home from his job at a fast food restaurant. A child poisoned by the bite of an insect foreign to the area, but imported unsuspectingly on a single bunch of bananas bought by a mother who had carried the fruit without mishap to the checkout counter, the cashier weighing and bagging it, the insect transported to the little girl's home and to her hand, death by banana. A couple killed on their wedding day when a rogue thunderstorm suddenly brewed while the photographer took pictures in the park, lightning striking the tree under which the newlyweds stood, searing them together forever.

What are the chances? What are the odds?

If freak accidental deaths could happen to other people, why not Maxine?

And why not in an elevator?

✧ ✧ ✧

Maxine hesitated at the mouth of the Arts Tower elevator, calculating the time she had before her class - not enough time to take the stairs - and so she stepped in. She had heard the rumours about the mechanical problems. Nothing too serious, a few students stranded between floors for five minutes or so, the shrill alarm alerting the janitor, who soon had the elevator moving again.

Although her mind told her otherwise, arguing on the side of rationality, her body alerted her to danger. Her heart and breathing rate increased. The elevator door shut halfway, then pressed open again. More people rushed in and out. Panic welled inside Maxine and she tried to leave, but the flow of students did not allow it and the elevator descended. Two girls standing at the front and smelling heavy of hairspray spouted nonsense, without a care in the world, as if death were politely predictable and did not arrive without an invitation. Someone behind her coughed. Maxine felt warm moist air against the back of her neck. If she didn't die in an elevator crash, she'd probably die of some vile airborne disease. She concentrated on the strip of bright numbers marking the progress of the descent. The elevator slowed to a stop. The ninth floor. She could get off here, she thought, push past the obnoxious girls, walk the rest of the way to the top of the Arts Tower. Better be late than dead.

The elevator doors opened to a jungle of thick wire and metal cords pressed against a concrete wall. "Shit," the voice with the cough said behind her, a skinny arm reaching impatiently over Maxine's shoulder to press the emergency button.

The hairspray girls giggled.

"I want out," Maxine said.

"You aren't the only fucking one," the voice with the cough muttered.

The elevator started to move, but without its usual uniform motion. It jerked, and then dropped, and then stopped again. A space opened up now, but only a crawl space, a few feet in height, defined by the floor of the elevator and the ceiling of the ninth floor. After that, more concrete and steel.

"Jump," voices urged from outside the elevator. "It's not far."

The boy with the cough pushed in front of Maxine. "What happens if the fucking thing starts up again?" he said. He moved from foot to foot, then bit at the skin on the side of his thumb. "Someone crawling through that crack? He'll be fucking cut in half."

The girls tittered.

"Chicken shit," one of them said, then hopped through the crawl space, followed by the other.

"Chicken shit yourself," the boy muttered, then moved to the back of the elevator and pressed into the corner.

Maxine mulled over her choices.

She could sit in the elevator with the jerk in the corner, breathing in his germs, for hours, maybe, waiting until the janitor

fixed the problem. She could crawl through the opening, either to her death or to safety, depending whether or not the elevator chose that moment to resume its journey. Or she could stay put, and die anyway, plummeting through the elevator shaft, because the elevator was really in much worse condition than anyone had imagined.
 Maxine was chicken-shit herself.
 Very chicken-shit.
 She felt paralyzed by fear, but also by her choices.
 What guarantees were there that she'd make the right choice?
 To jump or not to jump?
 Action or reticence?

✧ ✧ ✧

You'd surprise yourself, what guts you'd have, when push comes to shove.
 Maxine got down on her hands and knees, peered through the small gap of open space through which she would need to leap if she were to escape. The drop into the lobby was further than she had anticipated, a good two or three metres. She heard a grinding above her, as if pulleys and wires threatened to move.
 Maxine threw her bag out of the gap.
 Her university text hit the tiled floor below with a thud.
 Maxine hesitated and the thought occurred to her that she should play it safe, stay put until the campus security staff arrived. But she didn't play it safe, didn't stay put. She jumped, and with the jump, time stopped - that slow exhilarating moment of heightened awareness, her arms spread wide, nothing holding her, no solid ground beneath her feet, no guarantees, just this glorious suspension, and the truth itself.
 When push came to shove, she had leaped.

CHAPTER 14

Ben looked up from his laptop. "Too much obituary on your mind. Wanna take a break and go to the Rotter's Club?" he asked.

"I'll take the obit with me," Maxine said, grabbing a sweater, happy for the excuse to get a break from homework death. "A beer might loosen up my brain, unleash my grim-reaper muse."

The Rotters Club was an underground hangout on Bank Street, literally underground, at the bottom of a winding grungy staircase in the basement of a restaurant. It was an underground culture, too, a place that stayed open all night and where kids lost themselves in the music, in the drugs, in the alcohol, in the dancing. Their friend, Elijah, was already dancing when they arrived, his untamed style of leaping about the dance floor, one moment with the insane kinesis of Mick Jagger, the next with the gazelle strength of Rudolf Nureyev. Ben joined Elijah and they bounced around together in their own otherworldly space, like matter in the process of changing form, electrons heating up, speeding up. It was mid-week, so the club was almost empty, and Ben and Elijah could expand their movements to take up most of the dance floor, their own private molecular space. Maxine watched amused, but didn't join them. Instead, she found a small empty table in the dim corner, under a dim light, pulled out her Sharpie pen and paper.

"Boo!"

Maxine jolted, sent a smear of black Sharpie highlighter pen across the page.

"Jesus, Elijah, you scared the hell out of me."

"Good," Elijah said. "You looked too comfortable, sitting there, writing away. Come, dance with us."

"Can't, Elijah. Got to finish this assignment."

Elijah hopped over the chair and sat beside her. His hair was plastered to his head, and his face flushed with the dancing.

"What are you writing? A poem?"

"You're the only poet here," Maxine said. Elijah had published a poetry collection with a small literary press. "Me? I'm writing my obituary."

"Ah," Elijah said, as if that explained it, that there was nothing unusual about writing one's obituary. "How's it going?"

"To be honest, it could be anybody's obituary. Nothing unique so far."

"Maybe you should come skydiving with me. Something to write about."

"Yeah, right, also give me a reason for an obituary."

"It's a rush, Max. You jump from the plane and sail through space."

"Try a better word. How about, plunge. You plunge through space."

Elijah laughed. His exuberance was catching. Maxine laughed, too.

"You plunge at the beginning," Elijah said. "But then you sail. You should take more risks. You're too safe."

Elijah took risks. Lived life on the edge. Then jumped off. Maxine lived life in the middle. Sometimes ventured to the edge, peeked over, took a look, then withdrew.

"You'd love free-falling, Max, if you'd just try it."

Elijah had this way of speaking not only with his voice, but with his whole body. To demonstrate his next words, he pulled his arms into his chest and hunched his head and shoulders. "If you make your body compact into a ball, you'll plunge." Then he jumped out of his chair, stretched his arms wide, his head back, and stood spread-eagled. "If you spread your arms and legs wide, you'll sail. You can actually control your direction."

Elijah lifted one arm slightly higher to show her what he meant, and zoomed around her chair like an airplane. "You can do acrobatics. Somersaults and flips. There are no words to explain the sensation, spinning through space, no words at all."

Sometimes, Elijah jumped with others. They'd jump out of the plane separately, then by controlling their movements, come closer and closer, until they touched fingers, locked hands. His favourite formation, he told Maxine, was a circle. They collectively resembled a bicycle wheel slowly turning on its side, their outstretched arms and legs the spokes. Their heels lifted up behind them, their knees slightly bent, their bellies parallel to the ground.

Maxine loved Elijah for his abandonment, for his ability to free-fall.

"When you jump, you push the envelope," Elijah said.

"What do you mean?"

Maxine was not, by nature, an envelope pusher.

"There's a point in a free-fall when it's too late," Elijah answered, rather casually to be describing death. "Even if you open your parachute, there's no time for it to billow, to catch air. Pushing the envelope means taking yourself closer and closer to that point, getting the maximum out of the free-fall, extending the sensation, the rush, to its ultimate moment. And living to tell the tale."

Maxine was horrified.

She must have looked horrified, too.

"It's calculated," Elijah assured her. "Very controlled, actually, a balance between ecstasy and restraint, experiencing the rush and watching the rush from outside yourself, losing yourself to the jump but still knowing exactly when to pull open the chute."

"I wouldn't have the guts."

"You'd surprise yourself, what guts you'd have, when push comes to shove."

Ben joined them, carrying three beers.

"Read what you've written so far, my little dead girl," he said, plunking the bottles down.

So Maxine read her obituary to Ben and Elijah, all three of them bent "tête-à-tête" over a small round table in a dimly lit bar, Maxine shouting the words to be heard over the music. The music stopped abruptly, somewhere between "beloved daughter of George and Golda," and "mourned deeply by her dear sisters and brother," the words loud and large against the unexpected silence.

"You know you've got to kill some of them off," Elijah said.

"He's right, Max," Ben said, guzzling from his beer, then putting the bottle down on the table, leaving one more ring on the tabletop. "Most of them, in fact. You die at a hundred. Do you really think everyone in your life will still be alive?"

Maxine was horrified at the thought, but also found it insanely funny, in an unholy kind of way. Life and death held in her hands, a few strokes of her Sharpie highlighter, and she had written off her family. A literary hit man. Rather, a literary hit woman. In the writing of her obituary, death hadn't occurred to her, none other than her own anyway.

"But who do I kill off?"

"Your parents to start. They'd be one hundred and thirty, and then there's always Adeline, she's the one with the short lifeline, and Peter does smoke like a chimney, surely lung cancer would have gotten him."

It was simply an exercise, a journalism assignment. There was no truth to the obituary. Maxine knew that fact intellectually, but at another level, to give voice to the death of her mother and father, her brother and sisters, even just literary voice, bothered her in a deep-down, bone-marrow way. She didn't want to think about her family's deaths. Surely, death was inevitable. Someday, her parents would die. Someday, Adeline and Movida and Peter would die. Someday, she would die. But all of that happened in the distant future. Maxine was still young, too young to have reached that stage in life where people around you start dying, too young to notice that her parents had reached that stage, a funeral at least once a month, a neighbour, the elderly parents of their friends, a co-worker. Golda and George read the newspaper obituaries not as a theoretical assignment, but to see which funeral they should attend next. And to see if they were still alive, George joked to Maxine. "Oh, you'll both live to be a hundred," Maxine dismissed the comment and the topic of death in general, one hundred years seeming to be the longevity target.

"Kill me off, Max. Write me out of your life. You know what the song says," Ben said that night at the Rotter's Club, breaking into a drunken version of "Only the Good Die Young."

Elijah jumped from his chair like a raving maniac, strummed wildly on an imaginary guitar. Even Maxine had to laugh.

"I can't kill you, Ben," she said. "Who'd be the father of my - "

She stopped herself before she finished the sentence, but it was too late.

"I'll be the father of your children," Elijah offered.

Elijah and Ben looked at each other and burst into hysterical laughter, like those urban-myth *National Inquirer* people who burst into spontaneous flames.

"What's so funny about being the father of my children?" Maxine asked.

Ben stopped laughing, instant sobriety.

"You're not pregnant, are you, Max?"

"I'm not pregnant. It's just someday, well - "

She assumed she'd have children.

"By the time I'm a hundred, I would certainly have married someone and had a family."

"Is that a proposal?"

"No, it's not a proposal. Besides, you're drunk."

"I've had two beers, I'm not drunk."

"I'll marry you in my obituary," Maxine said. "Beloved wife of Ben Barlow."

"That makes you Maxine Barlow."

"I kept my maiden name, remained Maxine Lane for my whole hundred years, an independent woman."

"Did we have a good life together, Max?"

"A very good life."

A while later, Maxine turned to Ben and said out of the blue, "I did that as a kid, the thing you were talking about earlier at home."

"What thing?"

"Cut off my oxygen supply, it was a game we played."

"Playing doctor, Max, now that's pretty much a game expected of kids, but auto-erotic asphyxiation."

"Very funny," Maxine said, shoving Ben's arm so that beer spilled from his bottle and across his hand. "I didn't play sex games as a kid beyond spin-the-bottle and a quick kiss behind the bushes, if you could call those sex games."

"What then? You wrapped a skipping rope around your neck and jumped off your bunk bed?"

"I must have been about twelve. A bunch of us were playing at the dock, and some new guy, don't know his name, started the game. All I remember is doing what he did, crouching down, putting my thumb in my mouth, and blowing hard until I blacked out. When I gained consciousness, I found myself chugging away on the grass."

"Chugging away?"

"Yeah, like a train chugs. It was the weirdest sensation. I was curled up on the ground, my body chugging. I can actually remember being on a train, the rhythm of the train on the tracks, sitting on the passenger seats with other people, in conversation with them, but not remembering what was said. It must have been an hallucination."

"Or a seizure."

"Maybe, but when I regained consciousness, I was absolutely certain I had been on a train. I wish I could remember what we had talked about, the passengers, but when I woke up, the words were just out of reach, as if they hung out there somewhere, if I could only grasp them, hold them in my hand, I'd know."

"Know what?"

"Whatever there is to know. I'd just *know*."

It had been like that for Maxine, just out of reach. Out of reach in terms of memory of the conversation, yes, but also in terms of setting, where in time and space the train ride had occurred, if in time and space. The experience had felt otherworldly. A peak experience, to use Maslow's term, the psychologist and his theories another bit of knowledge Maxine gleaned from her university education. But it wasn't a wild "Eureka"! Rather, it was calm and cool, the edge of death, almost cold comfort. The terrain, a train. The conversation, reasoned.

CHAPTER 15

It was one of Maxine's favourite memories of Ben; that, and him dancing with Elijah at the Rotter's Club. There was Ben standing in the very centre of the studio apartment plugged into his iPod, earphone wires dangling from his ears, slowly spinning, while the zebra finch flew huge circles around his head, large wild precise daring orbits. Ben in his own little universe. Maxine's pet bird swooping around the perimeter of the apartment, skilfully darting around the hanging lamp, curving into the corner, buzzing closer and closer to Ben's head, so close he must have felt the rush of wind from air displaced. It was a game they played, if it can be said birds have a sense of play. Maxine and Ben liked to think it was a game, anyway. The fact that Ben played the game at all, and then that he played it so intently, with such respect for the bird, made her love him even more – two equal bits of existence spinning about her apartment.

"Why would the pet store give Linda a bird for free?" Maxine asked Golda when her mother pawned the bird off on her.

"Because it's so ugly, nobody in their right mind would pay for it. And it's a mean son of a bird, a real scrapper, fought with all the others in its cage. Took out a budgie four times its size. That's how it lost an eye."

"You didn't tell me it was a one-eyed bird."

"Well, it is. If you don't take it, I don't know what will become of the poor thing. Suppose Linda will just open the cage door and let it go, although I can't imagine it surviving our winter. It's an Australian species of finch."

Golda already knew Maxine would take the bird. The conversation was merely the set-up. Maxine could not *not* rescue it, she was incapable of inaction in this situation. She'd feel sorry for it, and be moved by compassion to keep it. She was, after all, the grown-up version of that little girl who brought home a mangy half-dead cat, and gave insects and frogs and mice personalized funerals. The one-eye bit was a sure-fire guarantee Maxine would become the owner of the bird that Golda's friend was hocking.

"What am I going to do with a zebra finch?" Maxine asked. "How am I going to get it back to Ottawa? Anyway, why is Linda now getting rid of the bird, after she got it for free from the pet store?"

Maxine's reporter's instinct kicked into gear.

Maybe the bird was sick? Carried bird flu, or some other deadly disease?

"Linda wants to buy lovebirds, Maxine. Some romantic notion, probably because she doesn't have a husband, she thinks lovebirds will fill the void. Anyway, she says she'll give you the cage, too."

So that's how Maxine came to be the owner of a bird, and not just any bird, but a very ugly bird. The bird's feathers gave the appearance of being constantly ruffled, especially at the top of its head. Closer inspection showed feathers permanently lost, probably from past scraps with other birds, giving the sparse look on top. The finch cocked its head to one side, as if innately intelligent, and if not intelligent, then streetwise. Maxine later realized the bird cocked its head to compensate for its lack of vision, to get a better view of the world. A bird's eyes are placed at the side of its head, so having one eye meant literally seeing only half of what there was to see. In this case, the bird saw only the left side of the world.

Maxine found a spot for the cage in the corner of the living room in a small alcove. She put music on for the bird when she left for university classes. But the days were long, and she felt sorry for it, stuffed in a cage all day, unable to fly. So she left the cage door open. The bird emerged, hopping with its head turned toward the left, so it could see. It flew in ever-expanding circles around its cage, always in the same direction, gaining confidence, establishing flight patterns it would repeat hundreds of times a day, until it had mastered the perimeter of the studio apartment. Given free range, the bird returned to its cage at will, usually just to eat. With this new freedom, it began to sing a wonderful trill that thrilled Maxine, and that seemed much too glorious for such an ugly creature.

"It sings like an angel," Maxine said.

So she called the bird Gabriel, after the Archangel.

Gab for short.

Gab the bird lived like that, with Maxine, for about a week. But then Maxine began to think about those long days again, when the bird was alone. She went to the pet store and bought him a mate. So there were two birds flying about her studio apartment, as if they owned it.

Maxine felt better, now the birds were not caged and lonely.

She still felt occasional twinges of guilt and sadness.

Sure, they could fly throughout the studio apartment, instead of sitting on a perch in a cage. But her studio apartment was simply another cage, albeit bigger, with four walls to confine them, no blue sky, no open expanse.

"We're all caged in one way or another," Ben shrugged when Maxine voiced her concern about the birds bound by the parameters of the studio apartment. "How else would you describe Earth but a giant cage? A pleasant cage, at times, surrounded in a warm blanket of oxygen, with rain and plants and everything else we need."

Maxine hung up a millet stick.

Gab, quite tame by now, flew to eat it before she had moved away.

"In a way, life itself is a cage," Ben said. "We're confined to the rules of this existence. Gravity means you fall down, not up. Linear time means you grow old, not young. And then we die. Can't get around it. Death. Who knows what happens then? Maybe we get a new set of rules, a new cage."

Gab flew to the top of the curtain rod, a synthetic tree branch. He closed his one eye and tucked up a leg. His mate flew beside him. She fluffed up her feathers to catch air, creating her own blanket of warmth, the air warmed by the heat of her body. She snuggled next to Gab and they slept, dreaming whatever dreams birds dream.

Gab and LaGorda stripped Maxine's favorite plant in a single afternoon. She came home from class to find the fern defoliated. A few remaining twigs stuck up from the potted earth. Gab and La Gorda (the name given to the female bird after a character in a book Ben had read) were nowhere to be seen. Maxine checked the window to see if it had been inadvertently left open, the pair escaping into the confines of the larger cage. The heating in the apartment was erratic, sometimes overbearingly hot, and she would have to open the window, although it was now mid winter. Other times, heat was non-existent and she had to plug in an electric baseboard and put on three extra layers of clothes.

The window was closed.

Gab flew out from behind the curtain.

Maxine saw that pieces of fern protruded from the pocket formed where she had gathered the curtain with a piece of rope to let in the sun. Dust bunnies stuck out, too, and other small pieces of material that had once cluttered the room. Excess fern lay on the floor beneath the curtain-nest.

Maxine didn't have the heart to clear away the nesting material.

So she left it.

Maxine also left Gab and La Gorda sitting on four little blue-white eggs.

Ten days or so later, Maxine heard faint tweets, an identical sound to that made by pressing rubber squeak toys. Gab and La Gorda acted nonchalant, as if nothing new had happened, their demeanor, Maxine figured, meant to keep her away from their hatchlings, to fool her. But they couldn't keep up the pretense for long. The faint squeaks grew into loud squawks over the week. Gab and La Gorda flew in a frenzy from their feed dish to the babies, regurgitating the seed into their wide mouths. Maxine mixed milk with bread, as suggested by the pet store clerk, and left the mixture on a saucer on a table. From then on, Gab and La Gorda fed the babies milk and bread.

The nest, as do all nests, grew smaller.

Gab and La Gorda no longer slept in the curtain.

There wasn't room for them.

Birds bulged from the nest. Heads with gaping mouths hung out of the curtain pocket and squawked for food. Gab and La Gorda refused, perched just out of reach, coaxing the babies out. One, two, three, four eventually joined them.

Maxine sat at the farthest point in the studio apartment from the nest and watched. The babies hopped and fluttered. They hopped and fluttered in scattered directions and without obvious control. One hit the wall, the other hit a chair leg, another managed to hop/fly to the top of an end table, and the other crashed into the couch. The parents hurriedly flew from bird to bird, chirping instructions.

"Whoever thinks birds know how to fly innately," Maxine said to Ben, "haven't watched the babies close up. A cat would have a field day here. A regular kitty heaven."

Finally in early evening, Gab and La Gorda corralled the babies towards the nest, urging them onward with their cries, demonstrating the hops and flutters of the return journey. One, two, three birds. Not four. Maxine waited for Gab and La Gorda to realize they were one baby bird short, but the pair disappeared into the folds of the curtains, oblivious to their shortcoming. With a bit of scouting, she found the missing bird under the couch. She waited, hoping the bird would squawk for food, alerting the parents to itself.

But it didn't squawk.

Didn't make a single sound to communicate its predicament.

So finally, after an hour or so of waiting, Maxine intervened. She put on a pair of mittens, and carefully scooped up the bird. She didn't touch it directly, having heard the parents would abandon a baby with the smell of human on it. But what to do now? she wondered. To put the baby back in the nest would surely disturb the other birds, sending them in a frantic tumble from the curtain pocket, scattering them throughout her apartment once again. So Maxine placed the baby on the windowsill a short hop from the nest. The bird would certainly jump-flutter the remaining distance, or Gab and La Gorda would discover it and chirp until the fourth baby found its way home.

The next morning, Maxine discovered the bird dead on the windowsill.

Exactly where she had left it.

Frozen to death by the drop in temperature overnight.

When the time came, Gab and La Gorda, being birds and therefore territorial, chased away their offspring. A second family soon followed, and the process repeated itself, a microcosm of the big picture, the evolutionary crawl of life towards the future.

Maxine caught the first-brood birds, not an easy feat, their having been transformed into skilled flyers. Catching them took her a full day. Then she had to find good homes for the birds. That took her a full week, several of her friends ducking out of a room when she entered it. If there was no time to escape a face-to-face encounter, they invented ownership of non-existent cats and claimed newly diagnosed feather allergies.

Once again, babies ventured forth from the nest.

Again, one baby did not make it back.

This time, Maxine did not intervene. She had learned her lesson.

She left the bird near the bookshelf where it had landed and went off to school. When she returned, the bird was gone. She assumed nature had taken its course and Gab and La Gorda had lured the baby safely back to their nest.

Three days later, she pulled *The Tibetan Book of the Dead* from the bookcase and found the corpse of the baby bird. Legs stuck out stiffly from its body, rigor mortis set in; eye cavities already empty sunken holes.

Maxine put the corpse in a truffle box, and the truffle box in a tiny pink plastic bag, tying it with a tiny pink ribbon. She buried the bird in the back of her freezer until the spring, when she buried it properly in the small plot of ground behind the apartment building between the early blooming tulips.

CHAPTER 16

Maxine sat on the floor, poring over the *Ottawa Citizen*, pages spread around her.

"Ironic, isn't it?" she said.

"What's that?" Ben asked.

"This old lady, what happened to her – how she died, that's what's ironic. It says in the newspaper a tree fell on her."

"Didn't anyone yell timber?"

"Guess not. The irony, Ben, it wasn't just any random tree in any random forest. That would be tragic, but not ironic. The tree that killed her was the very same tree that her father planted a century earlier to celebrate her birth. That tree marked the birth of her, and the death of her. Think of it!"

Think of it, Maxine did.

Not in words, for once, but photographic images. Photo flashes clicked across the digital camera of her mind, the synapses of her brain firing like the rapid eye movement of a dream. Images in rapid succession, rapid review, the *click click click* of the camera, freeze-capturing the unfolding of a life. The exuberant new father in a sleeveless undershirt, the kind that men wore long ago, a shovel gripped in his hands, the sun bearing down *click* he pushes a boot against the flat edge of the metal shovel, pierces the earth *click* kneels over, eases the sapling into the hole to mark the birth of a child, the knotted root-ball cradled in his hands *click* throws dirt into the open spaces, the soil caught mid-air *click click click* a child crawls *click* and then walks *click* and then runs *click* grows strong of limb as the tree grows strong of limb. She plays with a doll beneath the canopy branches *click* her first puppy *click* leans her back against the trunk to write secrets in her diary *click* a first kiss under the dark night leaves *click click click* and life goes on, always on, the trunk rings counting the years. The leaves of the tree soft-green and small with spring budding *click* love, a marriage, the woman burgeoning with child, her features slipping into Maxine's features, Maxine burgeoning, images and identities and time periods and things that never were mixing like watercolours, the one constant the tree, large and lush and full *click* Maxine and Ben, their first child, their second in a stroller, and life repeats itself, children and grandchildren, a string of monumental events interspersed among the daily happenings *click click click*.

"What could be a safer bet than planting a sapling to mark the birth of your child?" Maxine asked Ben. "Who'd ever think you were planting the instrument of your baby's death?"

"Death gets everyone, Max. For her it was a rotting tree."

"It's like Gab and LaGorda's babies, the ones that didn't make it back to the nest. Leave the baby where it is, and it dies. Intervene, and the bird still dies. You'd think you were doing a good thing, planting a tree."

"There's no blueprint. You want a blueprint?"

"Yeah, I want a blueprint."

Maxine turned the page of the newspaper, scanned the headlines.

"Do you think things happen for a reason, Ben? I mean, this whole lady's life led to the exact point in time where she stood under that tree when it fell. In a way, the tree was led to that exact point, too, rotted to the precise extent that when she sat under its branches on the celebration of her hundredth birthday, the tree fell. Not a day before, not a day later, but that exact moment."

"Hey, maybe it was murder, Max. An ungrateful son, now an old man himself, sick of waiting for his inheritance, sick of waiting for the old lady to give up the ghost. Maybe he took an axe, and cut a small notch in the rotting tree trunk, set his mother's lawn chair next to the trunk, and at the right moment, when she was seated in it, leaned against the trunk from the other side."

"You think?"

"Nah, not really, more likely an accident. The old lady was simply in the wrong place at the wrong time. Bad luck. But then again, how would I know?"

"So sometimes the penny's lucky and sometimes it's not," Maxine answered, speaking more to herself than to Ben.

Sometimes the penny is lucky. Sometimes it is not.

Or it's snot, as Maxine's brother, Peter, was fond of saying, slurring together his words with such a flourish. Thrills, little Maxi would answer, tossing her long blond hair to the side with a flip of her head.

Those were the days.

✧ ✧ ✧

Penny, penny, bring me luck, before I stop to pick you up. Such a simple rhyme. Nice steady beat. Good for turning rope, skipping down the sidewalk, singing away without a worry in the world. Just like Maggie Muggins, the heroine in the first story Maxi had read on her own, a story no kid her own age had heard about, the dusty-paged book a literary relic from Golda's childhood library. Maggie Muggins, with her copper freckles, almost as big as pennies, if not as big then at least the same colour, her long brown braids flapping behind her like kite tails. Maggie Muggins, singing and skipping down the cobbled path at the end of every story. Maxi would come to the last page, and then shut the book, and feel content and warm and safe and complete, knowing in

her heart of hearts that Maggie Muggins still skipped down that cobbled path, exactly the way Maxine had envisioned it. No Big Bad Wolf to stalk Maggie Muggins, to follow her through the woods on the way to Grandmother's house.
That was a different book.
Another story.
Another little girl.
When Maxi spotted the penny on her way to the Easter egg hunt, spotted the penny on the sidewalk, shiny and new, she had bent to pick it up, saying the rhyme first, *Penny, penny, bring me luck, before I stop to pick you up.*
She felt very lucky.
After all, she had found a penny, hadn't she?
She skipped her way to the school grounds, where the Easter egg hunt was being held. Golda had let her travel the distance by herself, although Peter would meet her there later. It made Maxi feel very old and responsible to be trusted to go to the school grounds by herself, but then, she was five now. She held the penny tightly in her hand and felt its luck seep into her. She believed in magic and luck, and things like that. She believed in Santa Claus and Tinkerbelle and guardian angels and miracles.
A lady in floral print and wearing a pink straw bonnet explained the rules. Maxi listened carefully. The Easter egg hunt went like this: when the lady gave the signal, a clap of her hands, all the children would scatter and look for little white peas that had been hidden throughout the schoolyard. The hunt would continue for one half-hour. At the end of one half-hour exactly, the lady would clap her hands again, and the children would gather to have their peas counted. The child who found the most peas would win a Laura Secord Easter egg.
Maxi had imagined the Easter egg hunt. Candy behind every tree, in every crevice, under every rock, hanging from tree branches, hidden everywhere. Instead, they would hunt little white peas, the same kind that Peter shot from his peashooter, and that grew into plants with little white flowers. She pushed away her disappointment. At first, the peas were easy to find, but as time passed, the hunt grew more difficult. Too many

children, too few peas. Finally the lady clapped her hands, and the children gathered around her. Then she counted the peas. She wrote the children's names and "total peas collected by each" on a clipboard. It took a long time.

"How old are you?" the lady finally asked Maxine.

"Five," Maxine answered, holding up her four fingers and one thumb.

"Congratulations," the lady said. "You won the Easter egg for the most peas collected in the five and under category."

Maxine smiled broadly. Peter hadn't won. Adeline hadn't won. *She* had won.

She clutched the penny in her pocket, her good luck penny.

She didn't believe in coincidence; at five, she was too young to fathom the concept. She did, however, believe in magic. Knew without a doubt that the penny had brought her luck.

Maxine's father believed in lucky pennies too.

Not only lucky pennies, but lucky dimes and lucky quarters. When George went for a walk, he kept his eyes cast down, scouring the ground for shiny hints of glitter among the old brown leaves or candy bar wrappers or dirt. "Spring is the best time," he said to Maxine. "Snow's melting, washing away the old snow and grime and dirt, exposing loose change lost as far back as the fall and summer."

Sometimes George would return home grinning from ear-to-ear and with a pocket full of coins, silver as well as copper. Once, he found paper money, a "fiver" folded up into a tight little square as if it had once been squirreled away at the bottom of a mitt. "When you're out walking, keep your head out of the clouds and your eyes wide open for loose change," he told Maxine, sharing what seemed at the time to be harmless advice. "It's mind-boggling to fathom how many people walked right over that money and didn't bother to look down at their feet."

George shook his hand in his pocket so the coins jingled.

"All those people with their head in the clouds," he added smugly.

He seemed quite pleased that he wasn't one of them.

George's search for luck led him to play the lottery.

He calculated his lucky numbers with the precision of a mathematician - applied an illogical logic to predict which six of the forty-nine ping-pong balls would happen to be in the right place at the right time, exact conditions set for those six balls alone to fall through the chute into place for some lucky bugger to win a couple million dollars, depending upon the amount of the jackpot that week. George spent hours at the task, working his special kind of numerology. Factoring in the winning numbers from the previous week, the birth dates of his children, the time and day he and Golda were married, the house number of their first apartment, their telephone number, the number of letters in his name, the square root of the total of kernels in a popcorn tin, or any other significant factor that caught his fancy. He worked the calculations and reworked them until six sure-fire numbers emerged.

Sometimes in the middle of the task, George would go out to the back porch, look upward, and be overwhelmed by the vastness of the sky. He'd try to exert control over the night by counting the stars, but he'd forget at which star he had begun and have to start all over again, until finally, swamped by the task, swamped by infinity, he'd go back inside the house. Then he'd throw his mathematical scribbling into the trashcan and search out Maxine, badger her to come up with the winning lottery numbers as if they resided in her subconscious mind. She had only to access them, pull them out of herself like a rabbit out of a hat.

"Give me six numbers," George would say, pen and paper in hand.

Maxine would pretend she didn't hear him.

"C'mon, quick," he'd prodded. "Don't think too much about it. Just whatever combination pops into your brain."

Knowing from experience that he would not leave her alone, that he'd badger her all night, she'd give him six numbers. And then he'd look at her dubiously, and say, "Are you sure?"

And she would sigh and say, "I'm sure."

Full of hope, George would wait for the lottery to be drawn.

He'd putter in the garden. Pick up stones, toss them over the fence, pull weeds, check the growth of the tomatoes and the peas. Watch the nest-building of the birds, bits of string and cellophane and grass hanging from their beaks like streamers from a kite. Baby birds peeking from the round openings in the birdhouses George put high on poles out of the reach of cats, the babies pulling their heads back in, then venturing out again. Becoming braver and braver, until finally they jumped and flew away. George all the while dreaming about the lottery and what he'd do with his win. Little dreams, little indulgences. Nothing big or outrageous, nothing earth shattering or mind-altering. No hospital wings built or rainforests saved. Simply gifts he'd bestow upon himself, those he loved and the occasional unsuspecting stranger. Minor dreams. Minor accomplishments. Somehow not diminished by the adjective, but enhanced by it. There was sweetness about these dreams, and bitterness, too.

George's dreaming was bittersweet.

A bit like Maxine's life.

A lot like Maxine's life.

George never won the lottery. Oh, he claimed a few minor prizes. Ten dollars here, twenty-five dollars there, once a thousand, but nothing close to the amount he had put into the lottery. He spent twenty dollars a week for twenty years buying lottery tickets. It didn't take a mathematical wizard to see he came up on the minus side of the ledger.

Golda scoffed at George's methods, although not his desire. Wouldn't mind winning the big one herself. Preferred bingo, however, to the lottery. Went every Saturday night. Sometimes won. Sometimes didn't. Came out even over the years, but to her husband, it seemed she won all the time.

"Your mother's born under a lucky star," George said in awe to Maxine this particular night. Golda had come home with yet another plus outing, twenty dollars richer than when she had left the house, George being at the moment twenty dollars poorer, his numbers eluding him that week.

Movida, the youngest daughter, was the last family member to come home. She opened the door, looked in the hall mirror, saw she was askew, tucked in her blouse, straightened her hair. "Why don't you just put your foot down?" she said to Golda. "Tell him he can't spend anymore cash on the lottery."

"And ruin his entertainment?" Golda answered.

That's the way Golda viewed George's playing the numbers. Entertainment. No different from a movie and dinner.

"Better than a night out with the boys at the local tavern or spending money on a hooker or having an affair," Golda added, surprising the girls with the reference to sex, if only sex of the alley or backseat variety.

Adeline blushed and left the room.

Maxine started to speak, then held back, as was her nature. She kept what she was going to say to herself - that Golda's comparison didn't fit. The lottery wasn't like going to the tavern with the boys, or having a good lay with a hooker, or conducting an affair. Those situations didn't speak to hope, and that's what the lottery was about in the end when all was said and done.

Hope.

✧ ✧ ✧

Hope is a four-letter word.

Hope is also a perspective.

A way of looking at the future, positioning oneself.

People who practice a belief in hope are futurists, not in the same sense as demographers or economic analysts who study trends, throw in a bit of guesswork, predict the future state of the world, write a best-selling book, and gather to themselves a cult following. Maxine was not a guru. She had no following, but she was a futurist by this definition: *she looked forward into time with hope*. Hope manifested itself in Maxine as a quiet quality that appeared briefly, flashed across her body, then disappeared. The way she held herself, the way she moved, the way she phrased her words, the tone of her voice. Even while pummelled by a man with such hate that he never *saw* her, did not notice the freckles splattered like grains of sand across her cheeks, the green speckles like flints of jade in her eyes; even when left for dead at the side of a dark road, heartbeat slipping into stony silence, even then, somewhere in her being, Maxine had still felt hope.

Hope took root early in Maxine's life, as is often the case with characteristics of personality. It first took root at a fair on a fine summer's day, the ground of being, bingo. Golda's game, ironically, when it was the characteristic of hope that Maxine shared with her father. Maxi ate candyfloss, sticky and pink and fluffy and shaped like a beehive. She licked the floss off her finger, stared with awe at the lady who made the sweet stuff, stuck the paper cone into the vat empty except for a few wisps of pink, whirled the cone deftly around and around the outer edges, candy floss appearing out of thin air, clinging to the cone, magically. What better lesson in hope for a little girl than that? Candyfloss formed from nothing?

Maxi wandered over the hill. She stopped at the pagoda where a jazz band often played, but now there were rows of long tables and benches. A man barked letters and numbers into a microphone, his voice loud and clear: B - 3, N - 35, I - 21, O - 64. Maxi listened intently. She knew her alphabet, knew her numbers. She could play this game. She sat herself at the edge of the bench at the very corner of the longest table. She tried to make herself small so the lady wearing the apron with the large pockets wouldn't notice her, wouldn't tell her to leave the game to adults, to go play in the sandbox or on the swing. Shiny new prizes sat on top of shiny new boxes, gleaming teakettles and sparkling dishes, stainless steel pots and crystal vases, silverware and clocks, glasses and bowls.

A voice yelled BINGO. End-of-game noises arose, shuffling and small talk. People slid their red disk markers off the cards and put out quarters for the next game. Maxi put a quarter on the table, too, and was given a card. Bingo balls popped away like popcorn. A ball descended from the chute and the caller bellowed B-1. Maxi looked around her. Some of the players slid their hands across the table to put a chip on their card. There are so many people, Maxine thought. How could she win?

Another ball dropped, another number called.

Maxine slid her hand across the table with the lucky ones. She had that number.

Someone's got to win, Maxine thought. Might as well be me.

The simple realization that someone had to win, that it could be her as easily as anyone else who had plopped down a quarter, filled Maxi with hope.

Not confidence, but hope.

In that way that happens regularly in the movies but seldom in real life, Maxi got a fairy-tale ending. She yelled BINGO loud and clear, collected her prize, a plastic punch bowl with matching cups and handles that curled so the cups could be hung from the side of the bowl. Maxi didn't play another bingo game that day at the fair, her last quarter already spent, but she didn't need to play again. She had already won. And with that win, hope had irrevocably entrenched itself inside of her.

CHAPTER 17

What is a ghost anyway?
No sooner had my otherworldly thoughts turned from the desire for enlightenment to a desire for personal definition, than an *Encarta World English Dictionary* popped into my hands, resting across my yoga-knotted legs and flipped opened to the letter G.

This is what I read:

"**ghost** *n*
1. the spirit of somebody who has died, supposed to appear as a shadowy form or to cause sounds, the movement of objects, or a frightening atmosphere in a place
2. a faint, weak, or greatly reduced appearance, trace, or possibility of something
3. a weakened or watered-down version of somebody or something
4. a faint duplicate image of something seen on a screen or through a telescope, and caused by the reception of a double signal or by a mechanical defect
5. somebody who or something that seems to exist but does not, for example, a name entered on a list by

Dead Girl Diaries

      mistake
6. somebody who is absent from school or work but who is recorded as being present
7. *See* ghostwriter."

✧ ✧ ✧

Parts of the definition were dead-on.

Maxine is, without a doubt, absent from school or work. With bureaucracy such as it is, Maxine Lilli-Anne Lane probably still exists as a name in e-mail lists and billing records, her Yahoo inbox stuffed with unopened requests for alumni donations and offers for penis enlargements and final notices of lapsing subscriptions. I could readily accept that Maxine's current condition, and therefore mine, could be the fault of a mechanical defect - consider her luck with elevators. I liked the idea that Maxine could be seen through a telescope, like a distant star, although I had no living proof that such observation was the case. If I'm picking and choosing here, I'd prefer ghost as the possibility of something – potential, or energy, or the future. And if all that applied to Maxine, then it applied to me, although by one definition more than the others. I *am* the weakened or watered-down version of the real thing.

I didn't know until I was dead that ghost could be a verb. But there it was, in print, and I was not about to begin doubting the good word of the dictionary, the writer's holy book. I could doubt the existence of God, the existence of a meaningful universe, but not the dictionary.

Here is what the *Encarta* stated:
"**ghost** *v*
1. to glide silently like a ghost
2. *vt See* ghostwrite."

To conjugate the present tense: I ghost / you ghost / she ghosts / we ghost / you ghost / they ghost. As well, I ghostwrite / you ghostwrite / she ghostwrites...

Put noun and verb together: The ghost ghostwrites.
Or another example: The ghostwriter ghosts.

"Hey, that's a good one. Have you considered stand-up comedy?" the Voice said out of the blue, a brilliant azure suddenly filling the palette of my surroundings, bottom to top, like rising floodwater.

"Get it? Ghostwriter? You being a deceased journalist?"

"I get it!" I said. "I'm dead, not stupid."

"That's up for judgment."

Then the Voice disappeared once again, a habitual disappear-er. I returned my attention to the definitions. *The spirit of somebody who has died, supposed to appear as a shadowy form or to cause sounds, the movement of objects, or a frightening atmosphere in a place* - that was the definition that Maxine and Becky had in mind their sixteenth summer of life, when they worked at Camp Spirit as camp counsellors and dressed up as ghosts to frighten the campers. Rather, when *Maxine* dressed up as a ghost, white sheet draped over her head and body, holes cut in the material so she could see out, although it didn't help much, the bottom getting caught around her ankles, and Maxine tumbling into a freshly-opened grave.

"You'll be giving the campers something to remember, a story to tell around the campfire," Becky said, Maxine unconvinced she wanted to play the part of a ghost. "Hey, kids love to be scared – look how they love Hallowe'en."

"It's the candy that kids love about Hallowe'en," Maxine said. "And what if we get caught? Aren't you afraid of that?"

Becky looked at Maxine strangely.

"So what, we get expelled? If that's the greatest thing you have to fear – getting kicked out of Hallelujah Sweet-Jesus Summer Camp, then I envy you, Max. I wish my life were that easy," Becky said, as if she knew things Maxine could not even imagine.

Maxine clearly understood what had just transpired between them.

Becky had given her the opening, wanted Maxine to ask about those things which Maxine could not imagine. Maxine chose not to open the dark room of Becky's secrets, where fathers enter in the middle of the night and rouse little girls from sleep. Instead, she chose avoidance, a form of reticence. She threw herself into the role of ghost, became the ghost, and then the moment for asking had passed.

Camp Spirit was a holy-roller Pentecostal church camp Golda had discovered when she went through her "Praise the Lord" stage. The camp was situated in a tiny hamlet at the edge of Lake Spirit and next to Cemetery Spirit, an old graveyard filled with sequential generations of the hamlet's dead. Becky was to wait until dusk, and then gather the campers for an evening nature walk, leading them along the garden path that stretched from the cabins through the flowerbeds, winding through a thicket of forest, and tumbling out into the cemetery. Maxine slipped away during Mess Hall chores, white sheet folded and tucked under her Camp Spirit T-shirt. Becky covered for her absence, completing Maxine's assigned clean-up tasks as well as her own, sweeping up the supper crumbs under the long rows of tables, and refilling the ketchup and mustard bottles.

At the cemetery, Maxine chose a large gravestone with a squat base to crouch behind. The plan: at sight of the campers, she'd gracefully, ethereally, rise from the dead, and *ghost – slide silently* – between the markers. Then she'd escape into the woods, chuck the sheet, and circle back to the cabins where she'd meet up with Becky and the campers, all aglow and trembling with ghost stories, and primed for the evening's campfire on the beach.

In position and with the stage set, Maxine pulled the sheet over her head and waited. Her calves cramped and she sat on the ground, stretching her legs, leaning her spine against the gravestone. The twilight deepened and a mosquito flew up under the white sheet. She swatted at it, hit her target, blood oozing onto her ghost apparel. A sliver of a moon, still low in the horizon but steadily rising, appeared in the sky. It occurred to Maxine, watching the moon and leaning against a gravestone, that she hadn't brought a flashlight. Soon she'd be engulfed in black night, and alone, at the far end of a cemetery. Where the hell was Becky? A bat swooped down and Maxine jumped to her feet, ducking and covering her sheet-clad head with her arms. "Look, a ghost!" she heard in the peripheral edges of her conscious awareness, and then, "What's it doing?"

Being still alive, Maxine didn't care about peripheral voices.

She ran, with no idea where she was running, since she couldn't see, the holes in the sheet no longer lined up with her eyes. She thought to yank off the sheet, but before she could turn thought to action, she stepped on the hem. Her foot tangled in the material and she tripped, lunging forward. She flew, finally ghost-like, didn't see the large gap in the ground freshly dug and waiting the morning's committal. By a strange quirk of fate, a weird kind of cognitive rehearsal, foretelling perhaps, Maxine found herself six-feet-under before her time.

Cognitive rehearsal.

In layman's terms, that meant getting ready for the real thing through role-play, preparing the brain and therefore the body, for the actual event, or so the experts called it in Maxine's *Introduction to Psychology* course textbook. And here Maxine thought she was just playing a prank on the campers, dressing up as a ghost. As for finding herself at the bottom of the open grave, well, that was an unexpected practice bonus.

CHAPTER 18

Did I exist? Did God exist? And what about Maxine? Was she just ghosting away, slipping into oblivion? And if so, would I just ghost away along with her? I shivered at the thought, but also at the drop in temperature. Suddenly I felt cold, not dead-cold, not heart-no-longer-pumping-blood-through-my-body-cold. Rather, damp and dank, Hansel-and-Gretel in the deep forest cold.

I looked around.

How did I come to be in this forest?

The same way I came to be dead I suppose.

Can't see the forest for the trees?

Perhaps it was the Voice speaking, I don't know. I couldn't trust my judgment - voices inside my head or outside my head, internal chatter or external reality.

There were so many, many trees, an eternity of them. They were enormous, no wonder I couldn't see the forest for the trees. Neither could I see the sunlight filtering through the treetops, so tall were these trees, so dense this forest. It was the kind of forest that Emily Carr would paint, fat round trunks so that if you put your arms around them, became a tree hugger, your fingers wouldn't touch. The trees stretched up until they disappeared from sight, stretched toward heaven, that mythical and unattainable state of grace. The forest was cathedral dark, and deathly quiet, so that even the voices inside my head, and outside of it, were silenced. I leaned against the trunk, the bark rough against my skin, the pine needles my meditation mat. I breathed in deeply, the forest somehow familiar, the iceberg tip of memory, the forest and the mist and the night thick in the way that sadness is thick. Wraps itself around you so you can't see the forest for the trees, can't find your way out, the sadness so large that if you put your arms around it, hug it to your breast, your fingers won't touch. But once in a while, once in a lifetime perhaps, once in an eternity perhaps, you find your way out of the forest, out of the elevator, tumble out into open space and blue sky.

I had hope.

Maybe I'd find paradise yet.

I don't know how it works, this otherworld, the laws that govern it. Like thought itself, events happened out-of-sequence, without logical sequential order. I'm in a coffin, and then I'm out of the coffin. I'm watching the Buddha get squashed by an elephant, and then I'm tumbling through space, and now I'm in a forest. And there I am, throughout it all, spinning like a slow top, planet-Maxine to Sun-Buddha, dreaming Maxine-dreams. Time and space and thought rolled up onto this tight little ball, all things occurring simultaneously. But to quote Golda, maybe that's just "bull," and there is only one event occupying its own tiny moment, this moment - Maxine lying at the side of an empty road, her brain shutting down, synapses exploding for one last time like the grand finale lightshow of the Canada Day fireworks. Blood pooling, body cooling, reaching that point in hypothermia where there is no longer panic, only soft peace.

"Paradise isn't all it's cracked up to be," I heard the Buddha thunder next to me.

"I thought you said Nirvana isn't what it's cracked up to be," I shouted back.

"Nirvana, paradise, it's all semantics," the Buddha answered, now sounding far away, a distant thunder.

I found myself curled up in the grass on the banks of a stream. Buddha was nowhere in sight, nowhere in sound. I padded like a puppy does before settling into sleep, circling his own tail, nestling in the tall grass to suit the shapes and contours of body. Then I lay down in the midst of these cool green pastures. I had finally found paradise, or paradise had found me. The Lord is my shepherd, I shall not want.

So I did what any dead person would do inside the 24th Psalm.

Rested in peace.

Paradise had no quality control, no standards to be met, no ledger with bad and good deeds tallied up and a final verdict rendered. I had expected entrance to be like a High School examination. A mark of fifty percent means you pass, a mark of forty-nine and you flunk, one lousy mark determining success or failure, heaven or hell. I was relieved to discover that wasn't the case. Eternity is a long time to be punished because you don't quite make the grade. It's not the murderer that you have to worry about getting a fair shake, the guy who waits at the side of the road for an unsuspecting victim, then bops her with a tire iron, leaving her abused and dead. It's the borderline, those who lived a series of events that weren't Mother-Theresa good or Jack-the-Ripper bad. The dead like Maxine; they're the ones who deserve the break, who deserve forgiveness and redemption. Maybe I had found both, forgiveness and redemption.

Perhaps even grace.

Paradise was perfectly wonderful, more wondrous than I had hoped lying in my coffin, trying so hard to find my way to heaven. A babbling stream flowed nearby and I closed my eyes, listened to the sound. And there I lay, in perfect bliss. No disturbances marred my paradise, no ferocious winds to send the stream into convulsions, no storms to blacken the eyes of the blue sky, no tremors to shake the ground, simply eternal peace. Only one dream occupied my heavenly sleep, that of the stream and the grass and the blue cloudless sky.

✧ ✧ ✧

Damn the stream and the grass and the blue cloudless sky.

A few millennia lying beside a stream, you want to get up and *do* something.

You want to *feel* something besides harmony and bliss and eternal peace. You want to experience each slice of creation relative to another. See the bits and pieces of existence rather than the unblemished perfection of the heavenly whole. Feel sweat stream down your face and spine, feel your heartbeat swallow you whole, feel the curve of your lover's back beneath your fingers. Feel fear, physical love, anger, sorrow; feel frustration, struggle, accomplishment, curiosity.

In paradise, there were no options, no variety of landscape or conditions or choice. No possibilities at all. In order for possibilities to exist, change must exist. Nothing ever changed in paradise. Paradise was perfection. After the initial rush, perfection is boring, perfectly boring.

A desire arose in the boredom of my paradise, a precious miracle, this ability to feel desire in a place as perfect as heaven. I yearned for a saviour, a renegade angel to sweep me into his wings and fly me away. To where, I didn't care. Any one of a thousand stars and planets and dimensions that must occupy the universe, any place where change is written into the formula of its existence.

Paradise is another word for hell. Dressed up differently, but still hell. I craved imperfection, a brutal wind cutting into my body as I struggled through the ice storm. Finally, finally, finally, finding refuge in a dark warm cave. Then, and only then, would I have found my paradise.

CHAPTER 10

Everyone is guilty of it, that one sin that would condemn the person to hell, or condemn the person to paradise, depending upon your viewpoint about what is heavenly and what is hellish. Maxine wasn't exempt in the sin department. She had her sins, too, sins that she kept hidden in the dark parts of her soul, that she brought out sometimes and placed in front of herself and looked at quickly, and then pushed back just as quickly, embarrassed and frightened by them. Oh, on the grand scale, she didn't sin often. You've got to put it in perspective. Put her life and her sins in perspective. Let's say, for argument's sake, she sinned once a year, the kind of sin that would prompt St. Peter to make a notation in the Book of Judgment. That's twenty-six sins written on her soul, her own personal Book of Judgment. Now let's say one or two of these were cardinal sins, the kind that would require a full citation. Not a shabby record, considering Maxine had completed almost ten thousand days of living, plus another two hundred and seventy days in the womb, and chalked up only a major sin or two. Not shabby at all. But a sin is a sin.

Granted, most of Maxine's sins were sins of omission, involved non-action, not that non-action is necessarily a sin.

Sometimes non-action is righteous, to use Godly language, for example, in the "I-want-to-make-out-with-my-best-friend's-boyfriend" scenario.

But did merely thinking about something that was wrong make it wrong?

Was thinking about a sin sinful?

Thinking may not be the best word to describe Maxine's preoccupation. Longing may be a better word, or as Golda might call it, hankering. Maxine hankered after Joel, Becky's boyfriend, and in time Becky's husband. Although Maxine never acted upon her hankering, never told Becky about it, never told Ben about it, or any other living soul, it was hankering nonetheless.

✧ ✧ ✧

Once in a while, by some freak of heaven, you get what you desire, a totally different concept than getting what you deserve.

"Bloody well wake up. You're the one who wants to be rescued."

I felt thick and groggy, a hangover-ish feeling, reminiscent of the morning-after, too much to drink at the Rotters Club. I opened my eye, and then opened two eyes, to be doubly certain that I saw what I saw. An angel loomed over me, large and glistening and sculpted, chiselled from marble. It wasn't his sight that startled me, but his touch. It was warm, as if blood flowed through his marble veins, and I realised in one swoop how much I missed touch. He brushed the tip of his wing against my brow, and I felt almost alive again. My heart fluttered, if that is possible, being dead, but that's the effect the angel had on me. He made my dead heart go a-flutter, and my dead spirit soar.

Then I hankered.

Golda would have been abhorred, my hankering over an angel. Adeline would have fainted, and Movida, my sweet baby sister Movida, would have lustily, lustfully, cheered me on.

"We'll sneak out through the back door," the angel

said. "The Almighty doesn't take kindly to prison, er – paradise breaks. His feelings get hurt."

"There's a back door to heaven?"

The angel shrugged, lifting his wings up and down in a way that made me swoon. "There's a back door to everything, part of the Overall Scheme."

"Overall Scheme?"

"Shush," the angel shushed, a long marble finger to his lips. "You dead humans are all the same, worry too much about intricacies, ask too many questions. Get one answer, you're still unsatisfied, and out pops another question. What in Hell was God thinking when He created mankind?"

I felt insulted, but held back my retort. This wasn't the time and place to argue with an angel about the merits of humanity. My escape was underway, and I didn't want to lose my personal Saviour, my rescuer. The angel hunched over, crept ahead of me through the long grass, wings wrapped around his body like a cloak. He took long strides, and I worked hard to keep up. We followed the stream through endless and monotonous fields of wildflowers and grass. It occurred to me just how ludicrous it was to sneak like criminals through the fields of heaven. The angel had wings. Why didn't we just fly?

"The roaring rush of beating wings - you want to wake up the Almighty?" the angel said in horror.

Suppose not, I thought, remembering biblical stories of earthquakes, famines, locusts and floods. "Suppose not," the angel mimicked.

Shit, he's telepathic, I thought. "Shit, he's telepathic," he mimicked again.

Now I was the one who was horrified. Had he heard my hankering? The angel smirked. I thought I should change the subject.

"Sure, change the subject, you're good at avoidance," the angel said.

"Have you come to grant Maxine redemption?" I pressed forward, avoiding his comment, which sounded an awful lot like a judgment.

"For what? A bit of red paint and a non-date?"

"I wasn't exactly an angel, you know."

"That's an understatement."

"The topic at hand is my redemption," I said, not wanting to be sidetracked.

"Then you're out of luck. I'm not in the redemption business. I'm a courier. I bring messages. It's in the Greek. Angel, αηγελοσ. Translation: messenger."

His words made me swell with hope, even if I was out of luck.

What message had he brought me?

The angel ignored my thought, pointed at a large mountain.

The mountain rose and fell like a giant stretched out sleeping on its back, and I heard a distant rumbling not unlike a gentle snore. I guess if God could be a burning bush, He could be a snoring mountain, too.

The ground shifted as God rolled over, sending a groundswell across the heaven-scape. We tiptoed around the Deity-mountain, reached the other side without mishap, without waking Him, and found the back door. The angel put his hand on the knob and then stopped.

"It's not too late to go back," he said. "To spend eternity in paradise."

Paradise was tempting, now that it wasn't the only possibility.

"Why are you doing this?" I asked. "Helping me escape?"

"Purely self-centred, you don't think I care about you, do you?"

My spirits plunged like a spurned lover.

"You try singing Alleluia for eternity. Never rock and roll, never the blues. Then never getting assigned to deliver the plum messages, the Gospels, or telling the Virgin Mary she's knocked up. I do it for the excitement, to see if I *can* do it."

My renegade angel swooped me up into his arms, rather roughly for an angel, I thought, too late to stop the thought. And in a beating rush of wings, we flew through the open door.

The angel's chest muscles expanded as his wings stretched back, and then contracted as they pushed down in flight, and I snuggled into his bosom.

"Know any bushes we could meet behind?" I asked.

He didn't answer, but that didn't stop my torrent of questions. "Where are we going? Why didn't you protect Maxine that night on the highway? Why is life so unfair?"

The unfair bit caught his attention.

"What makes you think any of this is set up to be fair?"

The words rushed from his lungs in a torrent that must have shaken distant galaxies, even parallel universes. Golda in her living room, one child less, surely felt his breath against her cheek, and drew comfort.

The vehemence of the response caught me off-guard.

Admittedly, I held a preconceived perception of angels, guardian angels and all, protectorates of the innocent, and those cute little Cupids shooting love arrows from bows. Sanitized angels, but there were also those four angels guarding the Garden of Eden, sentries staring unswervingly into the four directions and holding bright shining swords, fiery and swift and unyielding in their mission to keep humans from re-entering the Garden.

"Surely there's some ultimate accountability," I pressed, feeling justified, considering Maxine's violent demise and all she had suffered. "Good versus evil, God versus Satan, the forces of light versus the forces of darkness."

"Maybe a balancing of the two extremes, but polar viewpoints existing separate and apart? I doubt it."

"What do you mean, maybe and you doubt it," I said, my voice rising. "Celestial beings are supposed to know these things beyond a shadow of a doubt."

"Maxine's death wasn't fair, that I'll grant you beyond a shadow of a doubt. You want fairness? Try non-existence. Better still, go back to the green pastures."

I felt outrage. Pure outrage.

"Let go of me!"

The angel obeyed, dropped me without any regard to where I was or where I'd land or if I landed, dropped me and kept on flying.

I screamed my outrage down through the ages.

✧ ✧ ✧

"How do you want to die?" Maxine asked Elijah that night at the Rotter's Club, sitting at the table writing her obituary.

"With abandonment," he said.

It wasn't the answer Maxine had expected. She thought Elijah might say he wanted to die in his sleep, or to die quickly of a massive heart attack – no fuss or muss – no suffering.

"What do you mean?"

Elijah looked at her in that intently alive way of his, as if she were the only thing in the world in that moment, no one else, nothing more important or vital than their conversation, this freefalling exchange of words and thought.

"I pull the ripcord, Max, and it doesn't work, the parachute doesn't open, and the back-up doesn't work either. The earth is rushing up at me, and in that singular moment, I know without a doubt that I have missed the last possible chance to elude death. I want to meet my death head-on. No regrets."

Maxine laughed.

"Head-on, that's the truth for sure, Elijah. Head meets ground."

"Then you've written the headline, Max. Either that, or my headstone epitaph."

"Head-line. Head-stone. Crushed head. Pretty funny in a demented pun-ny way. But be honest with me Elijah. Death is theoretical, sitting here at the Rotter's Club with a beer in front of you. When it's time, and it's staring you in the face, how can you not regret your own death, especially in that last moment? No one wants to die."

"There are five-and-a-half billion individuals on the

planet. Surely there's at least one person on this planet who wants to die."

"You know what I mean, Elijah."

"Yeah, I do. *You* don't want to die. C'mon, Max, dance with me. You think too much."

Elijah grabbed Maxine by the hand, pulled her. She resisted, but only momentarily, and then not very strongly, leaving the obituary sitting on the table, the Sharpie fine-point highlighter rolling off the edge of the tabletop, the floor rushing up toward it. She joined Elijah and Ben on the dance floor and danced with uncharacteristic abandonment.

When the song ended and it came time to write the next section of her obituary, Maxine couldn't find her Sharpie highlighter. She crawled on all fours under the table at the Rotter's. She reluctantly gave up the search. Her desire to get the words out of her head and onto the page before they dissipated outweighed her desire to find her pen, but not by much. The Sharpie was her favourite, after all. Maxine brushed the dust off her clothes and dug around in her bag. Pulled out a tube of lipstick, tossed it back in the bag, felt around the bottom again, fished out a pencil and then wrote ferociously.

Ben leaned over her, brushed the webs and dust from her hair.

"The cobwebs in your hair are a nice touch, Max. Quite Goth. Matches the dead-girl doodles on the page."

"Golda would have been proud of me," Maxine said, ignoring the dead girl comments, but spontaneously shivering at the thought of the cobwebs. "Mid-career I was awarded the International Women's Media Foundation Courage in Journalism Award, which honors women who have shown extraordinary strength of character and integrity while reporting the news under danger and difficult situations. Golda always wanted a daughter dodging bullets in the thick of the journalistic fray."

"So you're writing your obituary to please your mother?"

"Hell, yes. Too bad she wouldn't be around to read it."

"Maybe you should give yourself the Pulitzer too."

"Can't. I'm Canadian, but I get the Order of Canada."

Maxine scribbled the award into her obituary.

Then she paused, gathering her words.

"Do you have any regrets?" she asked Ben.

Ben thought she was asking for reassurance, that she wanted him to say he didn't regret their relationship. That wasn't what she meant. She wanted to know if he had regretted past actions, things he had done that upon hindsight he would do differently, if he could.

"No regrets. You know I love you, Max. More than life itself."

Ben reached for his jacket, waved goodbye to Elijah, still bopping around the dance floor by himself, in his own private world. "C'mon, my favourite little dead girl," he said. "Pack up your diaries, let's go home."

CHAPTER 20

When Maxi was a small girl, and her sister Movida was a smaller girl, Movida would hide behind the living room curtain, or the bedroom door, or the big potted fern in the corner. She must have crouched there forever, forever in little girl terms, waiting for Maxi to skip down the hallway in that way that was Maxi, oblivious to all else, in her own little world, a naively cheerful Maggie Muggins. And just as Maxi passed by, Movida would pounce at her unexpectedly, gleefully springing up and yelling "Boo," like a deranged jack-in-the-box. Maxi would scream, long and loud, long and loud even after she knew it was Movida, and then she would cry. Golda would scold Movida for frightening her big sister and make them kiss, and Movida would promise never to do it again. And time would pass and Maxine would forget herself, and skip down the hallway and little Movida would lie in waiting.

"Why did you jump out at me like that?" Maxine asked Movida one day when they were both grown-up, or as grown-up as they could be, one of them a university student, and the other a teenaged mother.

Movida fed Pablum to her son, Jeffrey. She lifted the spoon handle so that it almost touched his nose and then slid the spoon from his mouth. Then she wiped the baby's face and repeated the action.

"What are you talking about?" Movida asked three spoonfuls later.

"That awful phase you went through, must have lasted a year at least. You'd scare the hell out of me, attack me from behind when I didn't expect it."

"I couldn't have been older than three, maybe four, Maxine, attack is a bit strong. C'mon Jeffrey, smile for Mommy."

Jeffrey didn't smile.

"You were so easy to scare, Maxine. Didn't matter how many times I jumped out at you, you'd still holler as if it were the first time."

Movida's child was autistic. That was the verdict of the small army of psychologists and social workers and other experts who administered the weeklong tests, all of which Jeffrey ignored equally, the tests and the experts. He sat unmoved, staring into the distance, never once distracted by their bright blocks and silly verses and nonsense games.

One day, he began to spin, whirling-dervish like, round and round for hours at a time if Movida let him, which she did after a while, since it gave him peace. "At least it's a deliberate action," she said hopefully, finding hope in the spinning Jeffrey had initiated. Jeffrey rarely initiated action, except when he was hugged, and then he'd pull away, strike out, hit if he had to hit, whatever it took to break the physical connection.

Golda cried non-stop for a week when Movida had told her that she was pregnant, although she softened like cheap margarine when she held her grandchild in her arms. Single mother by choice, Movida called it, refusing to name the father, abort the fetus or give up her son for adoption. So she lived on meagre government subsidies in a tiny apartment and managed, all at the tender age of nineteen.

You couldn't immediately tell Jeffrey was different. He wasn't violent, didn't scream or hit or bite or throw temper tantrums. He didn't have an over-sized head or abnormal features. He didn't use a wheelchair or have a physical defect. He didn't show symptoms of Tourette Syndrome, didn't have tics or curse a blue streak, didn't have seizures. Any one of these actions, or even a combination of them, might have made it easier, something tangible upon which to focus, to make Jeffrey's disability more real. Instead, he was a handsome boy with huge beautiful brown eyes, the kind that look permanently sad. He didn't fuss much, not even when his diaper was wet. He was never colicky, slept right through the night by two months of age.

Movida did say that it had struck her as odd, one evening, when she tiptoed into her son's room, so careful not to disturb him, peeked over the crib, and there he was, lying on his back, staring straight up at the ceiling, eyes wide, nary a peep. No arms outstretched, no *Pick me up Mommy*, no whimper of protest when she turned her back to him, and left the room.

"I often think about that moment," Movida said to Maxine. "It haunts me. What if it was a turning point, a pinprick in time that changed everything? If I had only lifted Jeffrey in my arms, didn't put him down, no matter how much he protested. Hugged him until he gave in, accepted it, and then reached out to me, hugged me back. Instead of turning around, and walking away. If I had only insisted - "

Maxine didn't know what to say or do, so she said nothing, did nothing. Didn't act, didn't hug her sister, didn't insist upon making the connection. She simply let the moment pass, a pinprick in time.

"Jeffrey feels it all, hears it all," Movida explained. "I mean that literally, every sensation. But he can't separate the sensation into bits and pieces, can't discriminate. Drowns in it. So to cope, he shuts down, shuts it out. Grabs the only lifeboat he has, that incessant spinning."

Maxine watched her nephew. He spun, just as Movida had said, a steady slow speed, round and round like a top. But there was another motion, too, so slight to be almost imperceptible. He rocked back and forth on his own personal axis.

"Either that, or he becomes mesmerized with one

thing," Movida continued. "Gets lost looking at a fly dead on the window sill, or dust under the dresser, or dirt in the bathtub, or a crack in the wall, or the pattern on the tile. Yesterday, I found him flat on the floor, dressed only in his diaper, bare skin against the cold tile, staring at the lines of the pattern."

"It must be hard for you," Maxine said.

Useless words, really. Stupid words, bland, non-committal.

It must be hard for you.

The words offered no solace, no emotion. Even anger would have been appropriate, wrapping her sister in a blanket of shared anger. Fuck-the-world, God-must-be-dead, how-else-could-He-create-a-place-where-children-suffer?

"Hard?" Movida said incredulously. "You think?"

Maxine started to turn away, but Movida grabbed her arm.

"Do you feel that, Maxine?" she asked, tightening her grip. "Does that hurt, like a simple hug hurts my son?"

Movida let go, but she wasn't finished.

"Do you hear the ticking of the kitchen clock, Maxine? Do you hear the bell ringing on the tricycle down the street? The squeal of tires, the slamming of the car door by the pizza delivery boy rushing to pick up his next order? The ambulance siren two streets over? Your own heartbeat? Do you feel it pound? Do you hear it thunder inside your chest? Jeffrey hears all that, all the time."

Maxine watched as her sister strode throughout the small apartment, turned up the volume of the television, turned up the radio until it blared Louis Armstrong's wonderful world, flicked through the songs on her iPod until Elvis Costello screamed through the speakers that the angels just wanna wear my red shoes, red shoes. Swiped her arm in one large expansive movement across the counter top, dishes and glasses and coffee machine and toaster crashing to the floor, the lid of the jam jar spinning across the tiles and disappearing into oblivion.

When Maxine asked Ben the question about regret, it was Movida she had had in mind. She regretted that she hadn't joined her sister in sweeping the dishes off the counter, throwing things, smashing them. Regretted that she hadn't flattened herself to the floor with Jeffrey and become lost in the pattern of the tile, hadn't spun like a whirling dervish with him, rocked back and forth in unison, the motion almost imperceptible, personal lines of axis parallel, if unable to intersect.

It is my regret too.

CHAPTER 21

George almost killed Maxine with his advice about loose change, the bit about keeping her eyes down and out of the clouds. Granted, he wasn't solely responsible, there was that lucky penny stuff too, but still, her father neglected to mention that she could get herself killed, stopping to pick up loose change, looking for luck at the side of the road.

Maxine and Ben didn't hear the sounds other pedestrians heard, the roar of the traffic, the swish of the city buses, the blare of horns, the wail of the police siren. They walked wrapped in that cocoon that surrounds young lovers, oblivious to every one and every thing but themselves, that air of non-attachment to the outside world, nothing-can-touch-us because we're in love, a carefree quality to their existence. Along Bank Street they stopped to hear a street performer, a young girl sitting cross-legged on a bench, singing folk songs and strumming a guitar. Ben threw a handful of coins into the open guitar case, and they continued their stroll, buying ice cream from a street vendor, heavenly hash on a sugar cone. Maxine licked the drips that slid down the side of the cone, delaying and savouring, while Ben took bites, finishing his ice-cream long before Maxine.

A copper glint caught Maxine's eye, and she looked

down. The voice from her childhood spoke delightedly in her mind: *Penny, penny, bring me luck before I stop to pick you up.* Then a voice-over of her father: *When you're out walking, keep your head out of the clouds and your eyes wide open for loose change.* For a moment, less than a moment, Maxine was the little girl on the way to hunt Easter eggs. She stepped off the curb, bent over to pick up the penny, and said the verse aloud. *"Penny, penny, bring me -"*

A bus whizzed by, so hair-strand close that Maxine felt the air displaced by its presence, air rushing around the gleaming metal frame and past her. She felt the heat of the bus, saw the startled faces of the passengers, knew the bus would have killed her, if she had stepped a centimetre or so further from the curb, would have thrown her high into the air, body slamming hard against the pavement. Maxine stood there dazed, the penny clutched in her hand. A horn honked, and a man shouted from his car, shook a fist. *Crazy stupid broad!*

Ben pulled Maxine up onto the sidewalk.

"What do you think you were doing?" he said.

"I spotted a lucky penny."

Maxine realized how stupid the explanation sounded.

"You almost died for a lousy penny?" Ben said incredulously.

Maxine began to shake. Ben put his arm around her and then pulled away.

"Do you realize it could have all been over just like that?" he said, angrily snapping his fingers together. "No warning at all. One second you're alive. Bang. The next you're dead."

The bus incident shook their faith. Oh, not faith in God, not faith in that sense, although it might have, if they had stopped to think about such things. Ben, in particular, showed symptoms of battered faith syndrome. Maxine sensed the change in him almost immediately. He began to look over his shoulder as if constantly on guard for a bus careening out of nowhere. He startled easily, jumped at the slightest sounds. He checked his watch often, shook it as if wanting to ensure time still ran forward, hadn't stopped on him or begun to unravel.

"I was so goddamn cocksure of things," he explained to Maxine. "But who is to say? Really say? That there'll be a tomorrow. The whole world operates on blind faith."

Maxine nodded. She knew what he was saying.

She was guilty herself, so cocksure that the sun would rise as it had always done, that time would not just stop ticking, that she would live another day, another week, another year, another decade. Grow old and sprout white hair. Have grandchildren. Bear children in the first place to have those grandchildren.

Ben definitely had it worse.

He couldn't get doubt out of his mind now that the floodgate had been opened. "Take this broccoli," he said later that evening when they were grocery shopping.

"Sure," Maxine answered, tossing a bunch into their shopping cart.

Ben retrieved the broccoli from the cart, put it back. "That's not what I mean. *Consider* the broccoli as a case in point. We come here and buy vegetables. They're not even in plastic bags. Who is to say some nut with a hard-on against the world didn't spray them with a deadly dose of pesticide? Maybe someone who walked in off the street, or maybe it happened enroute, or at the broccoli farm. How about that?"

"I suppose - "

"Or take the water supply. *Consider* the water supply. We assume it comes from our taps safe to drink. But how do we know for sure? Before we take the potentially deadly sip? Wouldn't that be the perfect terrorist act? Hold the world hostage by poisoning the water?"

"We could buy bottled," Maxine said, trying to lighten up the situation.

Ben didn't smile. Just continued. "You go to the restaurant. *Consider* the cook spits in your food, just for spite, and the waiter delivers it to you, and you eat the food, and catch a deadly disease, through no fault of your own."

Maxine pushed the cart away from the vegetable section, moved into the frozen desserts aisle. Ben followed closely behind. "We make so many assumptions, Max. Every day. We're so fucking trusting. There's this system set up, and we've fooled ourselves into thinking it's reliable, that the infrastructure won't collapse in shambles all around us sometime, even tomorrow, or in the next hour, or a split second into the future."

Maxine opened the freezer door. A blast of cold air hit her. She reached into the freezer, picked a Sara Lee frozen cake from the shelf. "The catalyst could be man-made, Max, a genetically engineered disease escaping from a laboratory due to human error, or cosmic, a meteor blasting a hole in the earth setting in motion another ice age. It's not unlikely, you know. The Earth is a sitting duck on a cosmic shooting range."

Sara Lee and roast duck for dinner tonight, served up with a gob of spit, unbeknownst to Ben. But somewhere else, in another part of her brain, Maxine wasn't amused. Mortality, especially one's own, is not a pleasant thought.

There were other bus encounters for Maxine besides the *penny, penny, bring me luck* variety. How could she escape them? Spend so much time on a bus, and bus encounters could not be avoided.

Maxine rode the bus to her summer job at the *Pennysaver*, a weekly "Buy & Sell" circular where she took phone calls from customers and wrote up their classified ads. The bus trip to work was an hour each way; that meant she spent two out of every twenty-four hours on buses throughout the summer months, longer if she missed her transfer, the first bus getting caught in traffic, or some other unforeseen incident over which she had no control.

The route to the *Pennysaver* wound from the inner city core to the commercial and industrial sections at the outer rim of the city limits. Twice daily people jammed into the bus, standing room only. On this particular evening commute, the driver crammed so many passengers into the bus he surely broke a city by-law or two. "Move to the back, move to the back, c'mon folks, we can do it, let's not leave anyone stranded," he belted out, missing his calling as an inspirational speaker. Against all odds, those standing in the aisle managed to move back a step or two, and miraculously, the entire clump of people on the street boarded.

The fellow snoozing next to Maxine bolted up, pulled the bell in panic. He crawled overtop of her and pushed his way through the throng in the aisle, starting a chain reaction of elbowing and jostling and bumping. Another chain reaction moved in the opposite direction, passengers shifting position, filling the vacancy like water seeking its own level. Maxine slid next to the window, stared out. She hated the bus, the stopping and starting, the crowds - not only the crowds, but the individuals on the bus, those hell-bent on individuality. The bus attracted them, a soapbox on wheels, a captive audience of passengers as hostage. There was always someone to bully, or to garner sympathy for a hard-luck story, or to hit up for loose change.

Most people living in the city, including Maxine, chose to be anonymous, did not draw attention to themselves, did not make eye contact with strangers, glanced down or away, as if looking at something in the distance, literally or in the distance of their mind. Growing up in a small town, Maxine never felt the need to be inconspicuous for the sake of safety. People greeted strangers with a hello or good evening, as if they knew them.

In the city, Maxine perfected the art of un-attention, learned from watching grandmothers with flowered kerchiefs and sagging bosoms and net shopping bags and thick shoes and drab dresses, old ladies shuffling the street unnoticed. Maxine translated the skill to the bus during rush hour. Be impersonal - not timid - that attracted attention, too, brought out the sharks. Rather, be inconspicuous, so that the crazies passed you by. Pass them by, too – don't stop.

Maxine figured there were two ways to survive in the city: be tougher than others so that they are afraid of you and leave you alone, or blend into the background. People are robbed or raped or knifed because they are noticed. Anonymity is a street survival technique. She didn't mind; it allowed her to be herself, or at least a part of herself. Riding the bus gave her permission to sink into reticence, to hide in the background. Familiar landmarks passed the bus window, landmarks not because of their fame or historical noteworthiness, but because they marked the progression of Maxine's journey home. The Carling Avenue strip malls. The Salvation Army Men's Hostel. The flower market.

"Watch yer fuckin' step! Those goddamn spikes are lethal weapons, lady. Government cutting into my freedoms by registering handguns, be better off registering high heels."

A few passengers laughed uneasily. The woman quickly apologized, probably half-expected the handgun to appear. Maxine wrote the headline in her mind: *Woman blown to high heavens over high heels.*

"The end time cometh," a voice proclaimed, this time from the back of the bus. "Repent or be damned."

"Ah, shut yer fuckin' mouth," the man against high heels answered.

The bus slowed for the next stop. The prophet left, no more revelations.

Maxine concentrated on the outside scenario, concentrated hard on avoiding the interior of the bus. The people. Their problems. Their prophecies.

But the scenario outside the bus window held life, too.

Too late now to turn away. Pretend she hadn't seen. Because she had.

An older gentleman stumbled across the green grass. The prophet, maybe, she didn't know for sure, since she hadn't looked at him, had kept turned away. But he didn't dress like a doomsday prophet, with long-hair and ripped jeans, wild eyes. He wore a suit and carried a briefcase. The man fell, first to his knee, then after a short pause, flat on the grass, stretched out, face down, motionless.

Where were the people to help? Why didn't someone rush to his aid?

Panic-stricken, Maxine looked around.

The bus slowly rolled into motion.

She hesitated, then reached up to pull the cord.

❖ ❖ ❖

Ben paced the front porch. His eyes were angry and wild, but something else glimmered through the anger. Maxine identified that something else. Fear.

"Sorry I'm late," Maxine said.

"Late is an understatement. You're *goddamn* late. *Four hours* late."

"I'm okay," Maxine reassured him.

She understood the source of his fear. He was afraid something unsuspected had befallen her. A meteor or a bus.

"Then where the hell were you?"

"At the hospital."

"Are you hurt?"

Panic, almost. Barely contained. She heard it in his voice.

Maxine sat on the step. The step bowed under the weight, too many years of non-repair, too many years of university students. She pulled Ben down beside her. "Not me, I'm not hurt. A man collapsed on the street from a diabetic coma. I got off the bus to help him, called the ambulance on my cell, and then went to the hospital."

Ben relaxed, somewhat. Then he puckered his eyebrows, resumed his worried look. "You got off the bus?"

"Nobody else did anything, Ben. I guess they thought he was just a drunk. That happens to diabetics a lot, or that's what Matthew said."

"You and this diabetic are now on a first name basis?"

The worry moved into jealousy. Maxine could feel the transformation in his body, the way his muscles tensed. She hadn't known him to be jealous before; it was another change that had happened to Ben, this new emotion. He had started to distrust not only the unfolding of physical occurrences, that the world followed a fairly predictable routine, but the unfolding of relationships, too.

"He's old enough to be my father. They gave him

medication and after a while he felt fine. A bit tired. We started talking. His name is Matthew Adams, and he's the publisher of a newspaper in a small town in the Upper Ottawa Valley near Pembroke. Offered me a job when I graduate."

Ben didn't respond. She put her arm through his arm, pulled him closer. "You should be happy for me, entry-level jobs are hard to find. I spend a year or two in some godforsaken little town up North, and I can get a job anywhere, move back to the city with experience."

"I was worried about you," Ben said. "Anything could have happened."

"I know," Maxine said.

And she did know what was bothering him, beyond her being late.

"Ben, I've been thinking about it lately, too. Life and death, separation."

He turned away. She thought he might cry. "We're sitting here, Max, on this porch, the sun shining as if it all makes sense. But it doesn't make sense, not anymore. The more I think about it, there's nothing you can count upon *for sure*, except random occurrences popping up without warning, popping up and hitting you full force, a slam out of nowhere."

The sun had begun to set, a huge round ball that dominated the sky.

Maxine shrugged.

"Then deceive yourself," she said. "Pretend there'll be a tomorrow, that the sun will rise in the morning, business as usual."

"You mean lie to myself?"

"Yeah, well no, not exactly, lie just a little. It's a kind of hope, but with bravado. Act like there's a tomorrow, Ben. Dare to believe it's true, even if somewhere deep inside you don't know. Otherwise, how could you continue? How could anyone?"

CHAPTER 22

Plunging through the ages, dropped by an angel and screaming my outrage, I thought about Maxine's statement: *Otherwise, how could you continue? How could anyone?* How indeed?

✧ ✧ ✧

You can't stay angry for an eternity. Sooner or later, your mood has to change, unless you're in paradise. So I screamed my outrage for who knows how long, an eon or two or three or four, and then stopped. But I didn't stop falling.

The way I saw it, I had two choices, right now, in the otherworld.

I could simply continue what I had been doing for who knows how long, falling without control, maybe screaming a bit louder. Or I could gather my guts, push the envelope. So I kicked back my heels, stretched out my extremities, flattened my body position, and soared. If Elijah could only see me now, I thought. If *Maxine* could see me now. Then I laughed at the craziness of the thought, my being Maxine, and all, albeit the dead version, the laughter lost in the exhilarating rush of my fall. There I was, freefalling through my otherworld and thinking about elevators, and Elijah, and the Rotter's Club, and Ben, and Movida, and autism, and regret, and luck and pennies. Funny, how that works, memory linking events and thoughts and emotions that seem so different, so un-linkable. Some quirky association is made, and there you have it, a connection. I suppose that's one of the elements that make a "human," one of the elements that separate humanity from the angels, who deliver the messages, but don't craft them. Humans stitch connections, like the carpets made by the peasants in the hills of Afghanistan, each carpet hand-hooked, and therefore different. You get an original. Every time out.

"Intriguing. But what would I know, being the lowly messenger?"

"You came back!" I said.

"That's obvious," the angel retorted.

He extended a wing and caught me in the split second before I smashed to smithereens, my being oblivious to the rapid approach of solid ground. My legs were weak from lack of use and my head dizzy from eons of free falling. I couldn't stand, so I sat on this piece of solid ground where the angel had placed me. My angel didn't stay to visit, no tea party with cookies, flew toward a snow-capped mountain ridge to the West. Rather, what I presumed to be the West, uncertain if the four directions had relevance here or if I mistakenly applied the structures of Maxine's earthly existence to this non-earthly place, unable to shake loose from her life - what she knew to be true, and of which I no longer could be certain.

White wings against blue sky. I watched until the angel was lost in the clouds. For all I knew they were one and the same, angel-clouds, a sweet and comforting thought. But like the living who accept without question that resurrection is all milk and honey, *Michael row your boat ashore, hallelujah* and then find themselves in an unlikely place as this, I felt betrayed by the next moment. The angel-clouds turned colour, swirling swiftly, darkly. Lightning tore open the black sky, as if God in His wrath had ripped the curtain of the tabernacle. A gale force ripped at my body, whiplashes of rain and sleet and wind. I dug my hands into the earth, took root, so to speak, so that I did not blow away, did not somersault like tumbleweed across the geography of this where-ever place. A black angry cloud hung directly above me, then descended, straight down, like an elevator, until I was immersed in vapour, my head in the clouds.

I realized with the plunge in temperature that my arms were bare, a fact which struck me as odd. I hadn't noticed the bareness before, couldn't remember what I had worn when I talked to the Buddha, or escaped from paradise, or snuggled in the arms of my angel. I had only a vague and dreadful feeling about what I had worn in the coffin, that silly peach Southern Belle dress that Golda loved so much, and Maxine hated. Hardly suitable for traipsing about the otherworld. One thing about dead people, you can dress them anyway you want for their funeral.

The peach dress was now gone. Thank God for small miracles.

Rain spilled in cold sheets and then turned into sleet, slapping against my skin. The miracle was indeed small. The peach dress had been replaced by cut-off jean shorts and a California Angels T-shirt. Perhaps my mirthless angel had a sense of humour after all. But I had no time to ponder the mysteries of the universe. How I came to be so clothed. I needed shelter, a warm dry place to weather the storm. I hunched my back and kept my head down, protecting my face from the sleet. My body stung with the cold, the sleet like a thousand little bites. And I set out. For what and where, I did not know, the place where my angel lived, I supposed.

I don't know why I didn't just curl up into a ball and go to sleep, give up in the midst of the raging storm. Die again, if that was possible. Commit otherworld suicide. Why not? What did I know with certainty?

For all I knew, the end of this otherworld would come with my next step, a sheer and sudden bluff, a bottomless drop from a hidden precipice. For all I knew, the storm *was* my eternity, and I was doomed to endure it forever like one of Scrooge's chained ghosts. For all I knew the future was far worse than the present or the past, a fate more cruel than this storm or death awaiting me. For all I knew the storm had subsided in the place from where I had set out, the sun melting the hailstones into harmless pools of water.

For all I knew.

The hail and snow were blinding. I could not see ahead, nor to the left or the right. I dare not look behind me, in case I turned to a pillar of salt or a block of ice. I tucked my chin into my chest and found small comfort from the cold.

Small comfort.

I meant those words.

A numbing wind blew through me, chilling me to the bone, if I did indeed have bone. I found comfort and warmth, however small, in the tucking of my chin. Strange things, small comforts, where we find them, in such unexpected places, unexpected times, like a small flower pushing up between a crack in the pavement.

Otherwise, how could we continue?

That's what Maxine had said that day to Ben, talking about life, death as the constant, the x or y of a mathematical formula, everything else in flux, uncertain, unstable, the chaotic raging of the storm. Maxine did that once in a while, dropped little round turds that ended up to be wisdom, not literal turds, but word-turds. Just little pieces of shit dropped into regular conversation that when examined more closely were astounding for their truth, or truth as far as anyone could know it, claim to know it. She'd be living her life, day in and day out, nothing much really, small sins and small accomplishments, tiny peaks and valleys, and wham, she'd say something or do something that made you stop and think. That took your breath away - because of its simplicity, its *feel* of truth.

Perhaps that's it, truth is nothing more than a fit, like a glove, or a dress, or a sweater, or a pair of jeans. You put it on, and you look in the mirror, and you say, Yes, it looks right, it *feels* right. I can live with this truth. Like that bit from Maxine about pretending. The more I thought about it, the more I knew it was true, that it *fit*, on a cosmic scale, as well as a human scale. Think about it: humanity perched precariously on a small piece of turf called the planet Earth hurling at insane speeds through the cosmos, part of an ever-expanding universe, where bits of creation push out further and further from its centre, like a stone flung from a slingshot. Add another spin to the tale, the spin of the earth on its axis, and at any one time an entire portion of the planet exists sideways. Yet, humans never feel the rush through space, the nauseous dizziness of the topsy-turvy planet. Pretence had been worked into creation. Time, and motion, and creation slow down in a cosmic feign to allow for life. I resolved to ask the Buddha about that, if we ever connected again, if I ever emerged from this hailstorm.

✧ ✧ ✧

"Ask me. I'm more qualified in such matters."
"Who are you?" I said.
"Albert Einstein."
It didn't strike me as odd that Albert Einstein could be here. If I could share the otherworld with the Buddha and an angel, why not Albert Einstein?
"It's relative," Einstein said, communicating in a bodiless way, as if he were a wave of sound bouncing off my mind, or a beam of light passing through a prism. A wave of sound bouncing off eternity. Is that it, Mr. Einstein? All we are? Nothing more real, more concrete, with no more complexity, no more body, than a wave of sound?
"It's all relative," Albert spoke as if in a classroom.
"Sure," I muttered, the dolt at the back of the class. "Relative, that's the singular of relatives, right? As in, say, sisters, brother, father, mother? Movida, Adeline, Peter, George and Golda?"

Einstein ignored my smart-ass comments.

"Have you noticed the cold while sitting here blizzard-dreaming about the life and times of Maxine?" he asked.

A blast of icy wind swept up the back of my California Angels T-shirt.

I shivered.

"Thanks Albert," I said. "Just what I needed, a dose of reality."

"You're welcome. What do you want? Right now, this instant?"

I spoke without hesitation, without having to think.

"Refuge."

A small dark cave where I could curl under thick fur of animal pelts, where the storm could not touch me although it raged outside. Nor touch Maxine, as much as I'm still her. Maxine deserved that much, a bit of refuge, since she obviously hadn't found it in death.

"Refuge, my dear, is only refuge in the presence of the storm. It's all relative."

The storm gave way for a brief moment, enough to let me distinguish a shape ahead. The shape took form, became a tree protruding from a rocky outcrop at the side of a cliff, boughs bent so they touched the ground with the weight of snow and ice.

I stood staring at the tree.

A single beautiful tree.

It wasn't simply an act of thinking, my understanding of this tree as beautiful. It wasn't an act of reason, where I logically, dispassionately analyzed the tree. I felt its beauty as revelation. It flashed through me, in a single point, like a jolt of electricity, overwhelming beauty in this one simple tree. I thought I couldn't survive, that my chest would burst, that I might die again, shrivel up like a piece of tinfoil set afire, curl up into a cinder, and be blown away by the wind. It's like Golda says: You can't look upon the face of God and live. Granted, this tree wasn't the face of God. Then again, who am I to say?

How beautiful the branches, cradling the snow, holding

the snow bravely, even gallantly, against the storm. I wondered why I hadn't before noticed the beauty of a winter tree, and then remembered that I had, as Maxine, the young girl a minor work of beauty, in her own way, on that day in her life. Hopping from foot to foot, trying to keep warm, standing safety patrol at the train tracks during lunch hour. Arms spread straight from her body like the branches of the tree, the children huddled behind her. Her breath escaping in vaporous clouds, her voice clear against the crisp winter air. "Now signs up," she sang, turning to face an imaginary train as if she really could stop it barrelling down the tracks. And on this day, after the children had safely crossed the track, Maxine had stopped to stare at a tree, marvelled at its beauty, glittering as if covered with diamonds.

Black lines of branch sketched beneath a layer of glistening ice.

Strange as it may seem, this single image, without the other million snapshots that made up her life, the million anecdotes, the million events, the million responses, the million sunsets and sunrises, this single image made Maxine's life worth the while.

So many trees on the planet Earth, more than a billion surely, add in a trillion plants and flora. People not noticing, passing through life as if wearing blinders, without acknowledging in rapt wonder each tree, each blade of grass, each flower, each leaf. Maxine, too. I marvel at the fact, marvel at the fact that she did not drown in wonder, that she did not die a million trillion deaths in the presence of a million trillion manifestations of life. The pattern of the scales of the pinecone, the dots of city lights against the night sky viewed from the mountaintop, the velvet cloak of blackness of a country night, the curl of the lips of the new moon, the silver flashes of a thousand small fish boiling the surface of the lake, the tick of the clock in the silence of the room, the peal of church chimes, the sudden laughter of unexpected delight, the burping of bullfrogs, a field of birds pecking at the grass then lifting as one, the sky dark with their flight, the turn of wings in the arc of flight shifting colour like the underside of a Venetian blind, the black line of the horizon like the etch of a felt-tip pen, sand hot on the soles of the feet, wonderfully hot, the sear of a paper cut, the acrid smell of wood stove in the below-zero night, the sweet smell of the shoreline, dead fish and seaweed, the musty smell of wet dog, so luxurious, you push your face into the fur, the heady smell of peony so thick it makes you dizzy, sweetly dizzy, an intoxication, the atmosphere pressing thickly against you like a blanket of rain forest, lightning and thunder splitting the sky, and you count the seconds, calculate the distance, rain pelting against your body, rain on your outstretched tongue, rain drenching your clothes, rain tasted through the pores of your body, and you are lost in the delight of sensation, or you should be lost, overwhelmed by the sheer wonder, by the sheer glory. Every time.

    I thought I might die, here, in the otherworld, in the presence of the tree, as surely as Maxine had died from the blow from the tire iron at the side of a road. It was a peculiar thought, dying from beauty, as peculiar as anything else. As peculiar as planets spinning through the galaxy, electrons spinning around nuclei; as peculiar as expanding universes, expanding consciousnesses, monkeys swinging from trees, children swinging skipping ropes, turtles emerging from the pond to sun on the rock, thought emerging from the pond of the brain to voice both nonsense and wisdom. As peculiar as toasters and submarines, evil and good, nuclear bombs and Jesus Christ, Buddha and gravity and sound waves, Albert Einstein and relativity and angels. As peculiar as life itself, heart beating, lungs breathing, blood pounding. As peculiar as all of these things, gathered up by some divine Hand and tossed into a big woven basket, the basket picked up and shaken, so that they mixed together in a tangled pile, like the contents of the thrift shop bargain bin.

    Memory so fine that it is devastating.

    Beauty so devastating that it brings death.

    Ego so overwhelmed that it can do nothing other than surrender.

    This is memory. This is beauty. This is life.

    I should have been lost, you should have been lost,

Maxine should have been lost, died a thousand deaths in the presence of life. Shrivelled up like tinfoil afire because we could not hold all of it inside of us, all at once, but died trying, died trying.

A worthy death.

CHAPTER 23

The snow at the base of the tree gave way. I dropped to my hands and knees, pawed at the snow, crawled inside the opening like a wild animal. I had found my refuge. The cave was small, and dark, and musty or musk-y, as if other animals besides me had occupied it in past years. The storm swirled at the entrance like a bevy of ghosts, shrieking and moaning like wind-notes from a wind instrument, sometimes high and eerie and flute-like, then dropping to the bottom of the register, low and deep and oboe-like. The howling of the storm was now sweet music to me, since I was inside the sanctuary of the cave.

My eyes grew accustomed to the dark.

I recognized shape, a pile of furs and a bed of fir branches.

I spread half the furs on top of the branches, settled in the middle, and then placed the remaining furs over me. Wiggled off my cold wet clothes, pushed them with my feet to the bottom of my fir bed. Curled up my knees, making myself into a ball, felt my body thaw, and then warm, drawing heat from the furs like a snake from the sun.

I wondered if the tree outside my cave was beautiful

because I had examined it in isolation, no other trees to minimize its beauty, this tree, the only such thing in the expanse of my otherworld. I wondered, too, if the tree were beautiful of its own accord, in an absolute sense, or if its beauty were dependent upon me, my interpretation of it as such. Then I wondered if this were true of Maxine's life, if her life had value on its own, without the surrounding context of events and thoughts and relationships and places and material things.

    I supposed it didn't matter.

    Regardless, Maxine lived.

    And regardless, the tree was beautiful.

    And this cave, right here and now, was my paradise.

    I closed my eyes, slipped into the peaceful sleep of dream and memory.

✧ ✧ ✧

It was wicked how Maxi's grade-two teacher could reach the high notes when she screamed. Wicked, how she could make her voice rise to the top of the scale so that it flew off the end of the register, like those dog whistles with sounds so shrill animals alone can pick up the frequency. Ms Ross, herself, was wicked, truly truly wicked. Hellishly wicked. How was it, then, that this hellish woman could be an instrument of beauty? What peculiar twist in creation set the stage that Ms Ross could carry Maxi to a place that was so exquisitely unearthly, even heavenly?

    The place where the angels live. That was the best way the little girl could think to describe it when she knelt on the floor at the edge of her bed that night and said her prayers and thanked God for Ms Ross. Never having met an angel before and having no real understanding at her young age of heavenly places, the comparison nevertheless expressed the joy and wonder she felt inside.

    "Watch out," Peter warned his sister when it came time for her to take a place in Ms Ross's classroom, the third in the secession of George and Golda's four children to do so. "She'll swat you with her pointer if you don't pay attention, if you even turn away for a moment, Maxi, SMACK!"

Peter smacked the table with his ruler and Maxi jumped. He repeated the smash of the ruler and Maxi jumped once again. Peter laughed and slapped the ruler again. Sure enough, like a puppet yanked by the string, Maxi jumped.

The first day of school, and forewarned, Maxi was careful to pay attention to Ms Ross and her pointer, the imaginary sound of SMACK reverberating through her brain. She did, however, sneak a peek at the piano that stood at the back of the class. No other class had a piano; that fact itself gave Ms Ross power, an aura that put her far above all other teachers. But after a full week of grade two, the piano disappointed Maxi. It stood large and majestic and novel, but did nothing. Then without warning, Ms Ross pulled out the stool hidden under the piano and sat down. She played a lullaby, the music soft and fragile. Her fingers rippled over the keys like wind over tall grass. Then she sang, her voice wrapping around piano notes like a morning glory vine around the stem of a hollyhock. Maxi thought she would surely die, the song so beautiful, Ms Ross's voice so beautiful, the piano notes so beautiful, that she would surely burst open down the centre and spill out like a milk pod spills seeds. She crossed her arms on her desk, put her face down so no one would see her red eyes, her flushed face. She felt confused that the song could make her cry.

That this, her first perception of art came in such a way, from such a person, was itself a revelation. That Ms Ross could scream so wickedly, in a voice so ugly, and then also be the *vehicle* of beauty, and even more startling, *be* beauty, taught Maxi this: life held it all, clutched tightly in its clenched fist. Violence and hope, evil and compassion, inertia and promise, and ugliness and beauty were inexplicably intertwined, like a bird's nest knit from string and twigs and bits of paper and cellophane, and sealed with mud.

✧ ✧ ✧

Maxine looked at Ben distantly, as if she were somewhere else, somewhere far away, and they couldn't quite touch, couldn't quite connect, as if their time periods didn't quite jive, everything a fraction off-kilter. She focused on his eyes; such beautiful grey eyes he had. She should notice them more often, notice details like the colour of eyes.

Then she remembered the task at hand.

The obituary. She was almost done, just a few more additions to make, fine-tuning. And then they could go to bed.

"So what do you think of Eve?"

"She shouldn't have listened to the snake," Ben said. "How like a woman."

Maxine threw a cushion at him, a wild trajectory that hit the living room wall instead of its mark. She did have that beer, after all, at the Rotter's Club.

"Not Eve, as in Adam and Eve. Eve for a name for our first daughter."

"First?" Ben said. "How many daughters did we have?"

"Two daughters and a son."

Ben picked up the pillow, pretended it was a basketball, leaped for the hoop, and slam-dunked the pillow on top of Maxine's head.

"Three kids. Isn't that excessive when the planet is dying from overpopulation?"

"Okay then, two kids, we'll only replace ourselves. A boy and a girl."

"Let's get started."

Maxine hooted. "You wish." She had moved beyond the Sharpie highlighter and death-graffiti stage, and inputted the obituary draft into her laptop for editing and final draft. "So Eve then?"

"Don't think so, Max. I wouldn't want to put original sin on the shoulders of a kid, even an imaginary obituary kid."

"Okay, then, if not Eve, how about Grace?"

"Like the state of grace?"

"Just like that. She'd be living in a perpetual state of Grace. What better birthright could we give a kid than that?"

"Amazing Grace," Ben said. "Yeah, that's good. Name her Grace."

Maxine inserted Grace into the blank space she had left, and then added Golda as a middle name to honour her mother. She would like her daughter to have a touch of Golda's brashness and confidence. Grace Golda.

Ben sat down next to Maxine on the couch, leaned his body against her body.

"So, Big Mama," he said, "what will we call our son?"

"Elijah," Maxine answered without hesitation, and then thought better of it. "If you'd rather name our son after you..."

"No, Elijah's perfect. Can't wait to tell him."

"And a middle name?"

"Blue," Ben said.

She didn't ask him to explain. There wasn't a need. It seemed right, the middle name of Blue for a boy named after their best friend, a man who falls through the sky with abandonment.

Elijah Blue, Maxine typed.

Then she hit the save button, and sent the file to print, and so their children were doubly immortalized - on computer file and on paper.

CHAPTER 24

Golda would peer out at them with psychic knowing from her owl-glasses. "Be careful what you wish," she'd warn her children. "It just might come true."

When Maxine first heard those words, she wasn't yet old enough to go to kindergarten. She spent that September afternoon playing in the backyard while Movida napped in her crib, and Peter and Adeline went off to school to suffer the yin-yang, beauty-anger of their teacher, Ms Ross.

Golda heaved the laundry basket to the back stoop, climbed up the bowed wooden steps, then strained to lift the wet sheets. She pinned the sheets to the clothesline and with a determined shove, sent the sheets out into the wind like sails on a ship. Maxi grew bored with her dolls and the polite tea party Golda had arranged for her next to the garden where the chrysanthemums and asters bloomed gold and purple. She wandered into the old garage, perhaps really an abandoned horse stable, its original use lost to the layers of years and families who had lived on the property.

Maxi stayed near the wide doors that opened up into the bright sun, and then crept deeper into the old garage with its spider webs and dirt floor and lessening light. She wasn't bored now. She felt something deliciously alluring that made her feel both afraid and alive. She stepped purposefully, her little body taut and ready to bolt, every safe and lovely thing she knew threatened.

It was still in her power to retreat, to turn and sprint for the open door, to go back to Golda standing high on the stoop and sending out the laundry, back to the tea party with her dolls on the blanket next to the garden. But instead Maxi crept deeper into the old garage, with each step knowing she drew closer to that point where there is no turning back, where the ground could open its mouth wide and swallow her whole.

And if Maxi wasn't a little girl in a garage, but a woman lying at the side of the road in the dead of night, gravel pressing against her cheek, she might say it was the edge between life and death. The line where the strange and marvellous quickening that moves your heartbeat flickers like a solar lamp in the witching hours, and you can't step back, can't return. It's too late.

That September day, Maxi somehow knew all that, like premonition, held it inside her with the freshness of a child's fear, in the way that only a child can hold it, with a clarity that becomes shrouded over time until you are grown up and lulled into a false sense of immortality.

Maxi took another step in the darkness of the garage, stepped full-face and full-chest into the sticky horror of a cobweb. She shoved the webs off with the rapid motions of a hummingbird's wings, and then found herself at the deepest corner of the garage.

And then the greatest surprise of all – nothing happened.

She stood there, breath held, waiting, but the ground stayed steady and solid.

Maxi's eyes grew accustomed to the dark.

A pile of wooden spindles took shape on the dirt floor.

Even though a black widow spider might have hid in the midst of it, she reached for the pile anyway. The fear she had kept checked became unleashed, tidal-waved through her tiny body, and she sprinted out of the garage, wooden spindles held haphazardly in her arms.

In the sunlight, next to the garden sprouting gold and purple, Maxi sat on the grass and caught her breath. Heart calmed, she wiped the sticky spider webs from the spindles with the napkins from the tea party. The spindles were carved, the kind that might have wound their way up a grand staircase. Maxi wondered what to do with them. She played until she found they fit perfectly under her armpits, that she could hobble like a poor little crippled child. And that's what she did, used them as crutches. Limped about the backyard with a gleeful woe is me. Golda looked down from the stoop. "Maxine," she said, using the grown-up version of the little girl's name, "there are children who are crippled, who can't just pretend. It's not nice to imitate them."

Then she added the warning that little Maxi heard as: "Be careful what you wish, it just might come true." But memory is a funny thing, elusive with no tangible existence of its own, and in reality Golda might have said something like: "Be careful what you pretend."

Then again, maybe she said: "Be careful what you write."

✧ ✧ ✧

"You didn't know where peas originated?" Ben said one night when they were cleaning up the table after a late dinner.

"The peas just appeared on my plate when I was a kid," Maxine laughed. "Abracadabra, open the can, there they were."

"You really thought peas came from a can?"

"Yeah."

"How could that be, Max?"

It surprised her that his voice carried an edge of anger. She had only related the childhood anecdote to amuse him, to make him smile. Oh, not full-blown anger, but there it was nevertheless, lying in the space between them. "I guess I never thought about it, Ben. Like I said, things simply appeared in our household, we never questioned the origin of anything, let alone peas."

Maxine tried to shift Ben's mood back to amusement.

"Jesus Christ, those canned peas Golda fed us were pure mush, moss-green clumps of god-knows-what, softened by that liquid meant to preserve them. Nothing fresh about those things, what child would have ever suspected that they were once living? That they were plants?"

Ben wasn't deterred. "Max, don't you see?"

"See what?"

"The connection."

Maxine picked up a fork, dried it haphazardly, threw it into the drawer. She felt her own anger grow. What did he want from her? "Sure I see it, Ben. I see the connection between peas in the can and peas in the pod. For God's sake, I see it."

"Deconstruction, that's the issue here. The peas come from the plant and the burger comes from the cow. It's ugly. Life is messy. Think about it, from conception onward the cow's sole purpose is to become a meal for you. They kill it, drain it of blood, hang it up in a meat locker, chop it into parts, wrap it in cellophane, ship it to the grocery store. You buy it, cook it, eat it, without once thinking about the middle steps."

Ben stopped, as if searching for the words to make Maxine understand, and then gave up. "Jesus, Max. Wasn't your grandfather a farmer? Shit, he must be rolling over in his grave right now."

Maxine stared at Ben, through Ben. She thought she caught sight of something just over his right shoulder, a shimmering like the mirages that rose on the highway when she was a kid travelling with her family to the beach, heat rising from the tar like ghosts. She could have sworn she saw a line of ghost girls dancing with an old man, hair the colour of a white cloud, arms linked, and then they passed right through the wall and were gone.

Poof! Just like that.

She shook her head, as if removing cobwebs, removing

ghosts.

"Do you think?" she said.

"Do I think what?" Ben asked.

"That he rolled over in his grave?"

Ben's anger dissipated like the wisps of a ghost. How could he stay mad at her? "If a dead man could roll over in his grave, Max, he probably did. Three times at least."

"I don't think he's in his grave," Maxine said.

"No? Then where is he?" Ben asked, reaching over to touch her face, his fingers lingering at her cheekbone, as if taking the shape of her face, the texture, the contour, into memory, an unconscious premonition of the end of things.

"Who'd stick around in a coffin for all eternity?" Maxine said. "I think he's off somewhere, line dancing, or doing a jig, a row of ghost girls at his elbow, accompanying him into the Garden of Pea-den."

Where that last idea came from, she had no idea, but she did have a pleasant afterthought, a thick green garden winding its way up from her memory, the feeling that it gave her safe and eternal. And if it were taste, as fresh as a peapod snapped off a vine and cracked open by big rough hands, the pea placed into a little girl's wide-open mouth.

✧ ✧ ✧

"Autism," Einstein whispered in my ear.

I rolled over - not in my grave - but in my cave. Heavenly, this cave, that's what it was, more heavenly than heaven. The storm roared outside, but I felt safe and satisfied, peaceful, even.

Except for the voice in my ear.

"It's a type of autism," Einstein said, more loudly now, as if trying to wake the dead. Given my circumstances, I should rephrase that - drop the comparison. Einstein spoke more loudly, trying to wake the dead. But the dead, this dead, didn't want to wake. I pulled the furs over my ear, but it didn't deter Einstein. He simply spoke in my head, instead of my ear.

"The ability of human beings to ignore phenomena. Think about life - rushing through space at breakneck speeds, spinning cosmic somersaults around the Earth's axis. Then throw a few other factors into the equation, say, the inevitability of our deaths, separation from those we love. Human beings choose to ignore all of that in the midst of living – as if it's never going to happen."

"What fucking choice did we have?"

Anger raged through me, so that even I was surprised at the intensity of my reaction. "What's the alternative to mass autism? Mass suicide, that's what. Self-destruction, death by too-much-reality."

For once, Einstein had nothing to say.

"How could any mother find the will to give birth if she knew her baby would die of crib death at six months, succumb to leukemia at six years, be bludgeoned with a tire iron at the side of the road at the age of twenty-six?" I screamed into the silence. "Life's a gamble, a crapshoot, and that's how we persist. An asteroid hurtling through space and destined to rendezvous with the third planet from the sun? Maybe, just maybe, the asteroid will miss!"

Penny, penny, bring me luck before I stop to pick you up.

I laughed wickedly, the sound of myself echoing throughout the cave.

"Hey, Albert, for all your brains, you were wrong. God does play dice with the universe."

God wasn't the only one who played dice with the universe. For all her university brains, Maxine forgot to renew the prescription of her birth control patch. Oh well, she thought, hurrying to the campus clinic to get the refill. She was only a day or two behind schedule. What was a day or two, anyway?

Forty-eight hours max, that's all.

What difference could forty-eight hours make?

She pushed the difference out of her mind.

Didn't bother to deconstruct.

CHAPTER 25

No matter how much she begged, Golda and George wouldn't let Maxi have a dog.

"Dogs are too much work," they said in unison, like a single entity. "A dog needs to be walked each day, and you can't leave a dog tied up in the backyard. It's not fair to the animal and then who'd clean up after it?"

Maxi didn't stop there. She pestered Golda and George. Finally in exasperation Golda blurted out the truth of the matter. "Dogs die, Maxine. Unexpected things happen. It might escape from the house and be hit by a car. Some dogs get sick, and then you have to put them to sleep."

Maxi must have looked confused.

"You have to make the decision to put them down. Give them a needle so they go to sleep forever. Do you want the sorrow of having to do that? Bearing that kind of sadness? It's easier just not to have the dog in the first place."

Maxi didn't want the sorrow of having to do that.

She didn't want to have to put a dog down.

She didn't want to put it to sleep forever.

That night in bed, Maxi kept wide-eyed as long as she could, fearful she would not wake up again. But eventually she couldn't keep her eyes open any longer. The next morning, Maxi was surprised to find herself alive. She patted her chest, her legs, her stomach just to make sure. Then she went downstairs in her pyjamas and Golda made her pancakes, drowned them with extra syrup. There was no more talk of a dog. The day proceeded as always except for two new thoughts, slipped between bites of pancakes, the syrup running down her chin and landing on her pyjama top.

Here were the two thoughts:
Did Golda and George ever wish they hadn't had her?
Was a life - whether a dog's or a little girl's – just too much sorrow to bear?

In the denial of the dog, Golda and George jumped right over the joy of having it to the sorrow of losing it. Jumped right to the end of the line, like the Québécois at their winter carnivals, skating across the ice towards a long row of barrels, back slung low, arms swinging, body gaining speed. Up and over the barrels they'd go, right overtop. And perhaps Golda and George weren't so wrong. Look how Maxi had cried over the death of Juliet, and she had only had the kitten overnight.

But like the tough skin that grows over a sliver, in time all that remains is the callous, the original hurt covered and forgotten. That's what happened to Maxine's family in their desire to protect. Their avoidance of sadness grew into a reserve. Call it reticence. Call it a space. They never let themselves close the space. Never got wonderfully messy, stretched out flat on the sand, grains of sand in their hair, in their ears, in their underwear, in their secret places, in their heart.

Bits of sand and seaweed clinging to their skin.

So Maxine became a journalist. Professionally, she lived in the third person. It was a place where she felt comfortable. A place where the space, the buffer, the gap, whatever you might call it, wrapped itself around her, kept her intact, safe from hurt. Kept her from firsthand. She watched and reported on other people's lives. Sometimes, somewhere deep inside, Maxine felt angry that she had believed the rules that had been constructed for her, had followed them all of her life, literally all of her life, the hourglass now firmly turned over, time free-falling through the space that joined the two worlds, the corridor between the living and the dead. Somewhere beneath the surface of everyday living, she felt angry that she hadn't questioned, that she had lived once or twice removed from the event. She had fallen into her life, rather than deliberately jumped into it.

    Or maybe I am confusing the issue.
    Maybe I am angry.
    First-person singular.

✧ ✧ ✧

"A death," Maxine said, after the fact, after the act.
    "I died."
    A death. I died.
    So those were the words Maxine chose to describe their lovemaking, much to Ben's chagrin. He had hoped for something more lasting, more living. Images full of life, full of colour, full of sensation, perhaps sweetness, words of love, not death. He hadn't meant to kill her, for God's sake. Just to make love to her.

✧ ✧ ✧

Maxine toyed with her food, toyed with the idea of not telling him at all. She reached for the wine, thought better of it, filled her wine glass with bottled water, smiled sarcastically at the irony.

    If she were going to have an abortion, what did it matter if she drank wine?

    She drew in her breath, as if she were going to speak, and then stopped, so that the sound of the intake of air into her lungs hung over the room expectantly.

    You're procrastinating, she told herself, thinking in the

third person. What's the big deal? Just come out and say it. Ben's the guy who gives the speeches about saying what you mean. He can handle it. Just tell him.

"Ben," she began.

Ben put down his fork.

Waited for her words.

But which words to speak, she wondered, at a loss. Which words to best lessen the impact, the confrontation, if there were to be one. She could take the humorous route, *Ben, the doctor tells me the rabbit died*, although she doubted he would know what that meant, a favourite expression of Golda's, meaning the tests had come back positive, an expression harking back from another age. Or she could hint at the state of affairs, simply say: *I missed my period this month*, or *I forgot to fill the prescription of my patch*, let him draw his own conclusions.

Baby bump, that's what they called it in the movies. A romantic, even quaint way to refer to pregnancy, as if the living breathing thing growing inside of you was only a "bump." A bump on the road. And then life goes on.

Maxine procrastinated one last time, reaching for the saltshaker. But then in a manner quite un-Maxine-like for its directness, she put down the saltshaker and said straight-out, "I'm pregnant."

Ben did not react in the way she thought he would.

There was no confrontation, no anger, no how-did-this-happen, you-told-me-you-were-on-birth-control blaming. Ben simply said, "I'll marry you." He spoke the words without procrastination, without first taking a long chug of water, without first walking to the window, staring out as if preoccupied, counting the birds lined up along the telephone wire, the leaves of the chestnut tree that pushed against the backyard fence, all the reasons why he should abandon ship, leave her, or at least let her deal with the baby bump without him.

Maxine found herself wildly and suddenly angry.

It was a reaction she couldn't rationalize, if she stopped to think logically about it. She looked for something to heave, a bicycle, anything. She grabbed the closest object, the saltshaker, and threw it like a missile, smacking Ben on the shoulder. Then she left the table, left the room, left the house, hurried alongside the Ottawa Canal. The lights of the parliament buildings shone against the black night, illuminating the roof a putrid green that made her think of pigeons. She passed beneath a bridge, the dirt path surrounded by large bushes and dark shadows, places for jumping out from behind. Her anger was so complete she did not think of her own safety, did not think of what might lie in wait behind the curtain, or door, or the dark highway of the shadows, thought only of Ben and his proposal. Not voiced as a question, Will you marry me, Maxine? But a statement of fact: I'll marry you.

What had she wanted him to say?

I love you more than life itself, Maxine, I can't bear the thought of living without you, will you be my wife, to have and to hold, 'til death do us part?

She started to cry.

What would she do?

CHAPTER 26

Maxine turned away from the coffee that sat waiting for her on the kitchen table the next morning, the smell making her stomach queasy. That was new – she loved coffee.

"I'm not keeping it," she said.

Ben didn't look up from his laptop screen. She wasn't sure he had heard her, no acknowledgement of the words. But just when she thought to leave the room, he spoke.

"It?"

"You know what I mean, Ben. The baby."

"So you're saying you'll give the baby up for adoption."

"No, that's not what I said." It pissed her off that he would rephrase her words. "I'm getting rid of it. Making an appointment through the university clinic."

"Jesus, Max." Ben flicked shut the laptop, picked up her full cup of coffee, emptied it in the sink. "So what was all that crap you wrote in your obituary?"

The obituary.

Maxine had forgotten about it.

"It was a school assignment, for God's sake," and then she added without thinking, without censor, "for fuck's sake."

"Well, that's what we've been doing, Max. Fucking. Like those peas in the can and the farmer's field – there's a fucking connection here."

"Fuck off," Maxine said, turning away.

"The boy and a girl, you even gave them names, Elijah Blue and Grace."

It startled her that Ben had remembered the names; she hadn't. She had received an "A" on the obituary, and then moved on to a million other requirements that had to be completed before she passed the course, writing the editorial, interviewing the witness, translating opinion pieces into journalistic blogging.

"I can't have a baby now, Ben. In the future, sure, but not now. I have that job lined up for the fall, a once-in-a-lifetime opportunity that might never repeat itself. We have a whole life ahead of us for children."

"We?" Ben said. "There's a *we* here?"

Three days later, Ben left.

He packed his duffel bag, shoved in his socks and underwear and T-shirts, took his toothbrush, rolled up a few pairs of jeans, grabbed a half-finished paperback from the nightstand, and made for the door.

"What about your other things?" Maxine asked on his way out.

"Junk them."

Maxine prolonged the leaving, trying to keep him there with her anger, with her questions. "The armchair, the coffee table, glasses, dishes, your winter coat, your runners?"

"Keep them, toss them, give them away, I don't care. They're just things."

Just things.

She caught the subtext.

Just things. Unlike a child.

"It's not easy for me, either," she said.

No more anger. Simply a statement.

Ben turned toward her, studied her. She saw him soften, thought he might change his mind, put down his duffel bag and stay. She wanted him to stay. The realization surprised her. She hadn't known it before this moment. She didn't want him to pack, to leave her. She felt this in the first person, felt it closely, as close as her own skin. Ben took the tip of her finger in his hand. Squeezed it, held it, then let go. It was a strange action, she thought, her hand hanging in the air for a moment, then dropping to her side. "I know it's not easy, Max. I just can't sit around here and watch you do what you have to do."

For the next few days, Maxine replayed Ben's leaving in her mind.

She became stuck on his parting words – *what you have to do*.

Not wish to do, going to do, but have to do.
Did she? What were the rules?
Were there rules?

✧ ✧ ✧

Sometimes, you finally make a decision, and life makes a different one for you.

That's irony.

Maxine felt a strange ping, both a sensation and a sound, if only a sound that she heard in her head, like musicians can hear the notes of music. The sound, the feel, was like the striking of a small bell with a tiny metal baton, and it reverberated, silently, the waves of sound spreading through her body. And then nothing else, nothing different, until the next day, when she noticed the tiny waves in her womb. She thought the sensation strange, unusual, perhaps nothing more than something disagreeable she must have eaten the night before, didn't recognize it for what is was, the start of labour, since she was barely pregnant, just a few months or so.

Five minutes later, she was drenched in blood.

She didn't know what to do, who to call, and then she did know who to call. Knew it intimately, first-person singular, like her own skin. She called Ben and then she collapsed on the floor.

She didn't know how long it took him to arrive; she gained consciousness when he shook her shoulders, his face laid bare with his fear for her. He helped her to her feet, half-carried her to the car, she leaning on him. He sped to the hospital, faster than the speed limit, perhaps faster than the speed of light, certainly the speed of sound, approaching a red light, going through it, careening to avoid a cyclist. As fast as they travelled, the journey seemed to take forever, time relative, not only in terms of external events, but also internal ones, the interior cosmos, events of emotional content. Finally they pulled into the emergency room driveway, abandoned the car, the doors wide open, Ben carrying Maxine in his arms into the hospital, her blood now on him, too.

It didn't occur to her at first that she might die. Lying there on the table, nurses rushing about, fussing now at her feet, Maxine's legs wide open, cloths to soak the bleeding, nurses now fussing at her side, checking her pulse, blood pressure, vitals, preparing her for needles, intravenous bottle rolled in and hanging ready, voices cooing, soothing, a juxtaposition, a discrepancy between words and actions. Ben refused to leave, crouching at the top of the table, stroking her head, her cheek, whispering, *I love you Max, Everything will be fine, I promise.* It occurred to Maxine somewhere in all that was happening that Ben didn't have the right to make that promise, but it soothed her that he did. *We can't stop the bleeding,* she heard another voice say, like a movie voiceover, and then and only then, did it occur to Maxine that she might die. She felt herself fading away, first her vision, blackness engulfing her, and then her body, fading away as if it were a chalk drawing that someone erased, bit by bit, first her arms, then her legs, then part of her chest. She couldn't stop her own bleeding, couldn't will it to stop, so instead she steeled herself, kept the panic at bay that wanted to swallow her, the sudden dip of the roller coaster. She didn't fight, rode the ride wherever it might take her, but not to death. Not today, she told herself. She would not die today.

Blackness.

Maxine awoke alone in a hospital room.

She wondered if she were dead, and then Ben came through the door, and she knew she wasn't. *The doctor says you'll be okay,* he told her. *And the baby?* Maxine asked. He looked at her peculiarly, as if she should know, how could she not know? *You had a miscarriage,* he said.

Maxine began to sob. Her body heaved, sadness washing through her in unrelenting waves that left no room for anything else. The sobs gathered into wails, and she could not stop herself, could not stop the grief. She covered her face with her hands, muffling the wails somewhat, but not her sadness. Tears pushed between her fingers, and the front of her gown grew wet, and then the pillow and sheets.

She wanted the baby, her want a secret she had harboured inside of herself, like the child itself. Had begun to believe it, that she could do this, give birth to a child, love a child, be a mother. Had begun to figure it out, familiarizing herself with the idea, gathering courage, fanning it like a spark of fire so that it would not die out, thought about how and when she would tell Ben. Maxine cried now for the child that would not be, cried for all the love she could not give, all the things they would not do together, all the happiness and sadness they would not experience. She grieved for this child who would not grow up, not grow older, not grow old, the child she would not know.

Ben came home.

Duffel bag in hand, socks and underwear and T-shirts, toothbrush, jeans rolled up, a half-read paperback, marked on the same dog-eared page. As if he had simply walked out the front door, down the porch steps, around the block, and then returned. But it wasn't just around the block – so much more distance had been travelled.

"Can I come in?" he asked.

Maxine nodded and so it was that Ben stayed.

Became the constant in the remainder of her life.

CHAPTER 27

Matthew had kept his word, gave Maxine a job at his newspapers after she graduated. She moved to Deep River, north of Ottawa, rented a "war-four house" - kitchen, living room, two bedrooms, that's it, except for a crawlspace for a basement. Ben came with her, worked at a lodge along the Ottawa River, shuttling tourists who had booked white-water rafting trips. On occasion, he navigated the rapids as the steersman to a raft-full of screaming, screeching, bouncing wannabe adventurers, but most of the time he drove the van and took care of the safety needs of the rafters – making sure they were all equipped with lifejackets and helmets that fit, paddles the correct length for their height and body build, and that they knew the safety drill in case of a spill. He loved the job, and particularly the rapids, had begun to talk about the future. His father had left him a bit of money in his will, and Ben thought if he were careful, managed the money well, did his research, paid his dues learning the ropes, he would be in a position to open his own white-water rafting business, maybe ask Elijah to be his business partner, at least work for him, being the adventurer type.

After Maxine settled in, had a month or so under her

belt at her new job, she called Becky. The banter felt familiar, so comfortingly familiar, like family, or how family should feel. She hadn't realized that she missed Becky so much these past few years, Becky living with Joel in Sudbury, where they had a baby on the way.

"How's Ben?" Becky asked.

"Spectacularly happy. Probably being flung around by rapids as we speak."

"And the new job?"

"The job is fine, Beck. Not spectacular. It's a good opportunity to learn. The newspaper is small, just like the town. There are few writers, so I get to do a lot of copy, from birth announcements to obits to front page news to the odd editorial."

"I bet those are odd."

Maxine let the comment pass, unable to think of a comeback wittily worthy. Besides, there was something else she wanted to talk about with Becky.

"The eclipse of the sun this afternoon. Did you watch it?"

"I value my eyesight. Stayed inside with my drapes closed."

"Beck, I'm driving and I notice this subtle change. Twilight is descending, and it's noon hour. Oh, not twilight. Twilight doesn't do it justice. It's a surreal mixture of dusk and day, sepia-tinged, like those old photographs. So I park the car and get out. The temperature has dropped, and the silence is eerie. No birds singing, no dogs barking, none of the normal country sounds. I look up, and there's a round edge of black eating the sun."

Maxine paused. The silence lingered there, comfortably, in the way it does between lifelong friends. Becky didn't fill it, waited for Maxine to continue.

"I had an interview scheduled, but I didn't care, Beck. Stood there wrapped in this strange dusk, staring at the eclipse, watching it elapse, the whole thing. The sky grew darker, and I could see the stars, in the middle of the day, the moon almost

totally engulfing the sun, and then it does, and there's this flash of light, a brilliant flash, and a dazzling halo surrounds the black of the moon like the outer edges have been set on fire."
More silence. Long silence.
Then Becky spoke.
"Didn't anyone ever tell you not to look at an eclipse?"
"All my life," Maxine said. "But I looked anyway."

✧ ✧ ✧

Ben and Maxine spent that last day together at the Pembroke Fall Fair. The next day Maxine would drive back to Ottawa to do background research for an article on the AECL plant at Chalk River, and its production of medical isotopes.
The two wandered hand-in-hand about the usual country fair stands and events, ribbons dangling from apple pies and jam preserves, a petting zoo where Maxine paid a loonie for an ice cream cone filled with grain which she fed, cone and all, to a billy goat that butted her for more. She escaped from the pen, and Ben teased her about the flight, billy goat in hot pursuit. Then they sat down under a big top tent to watch a step-dancing and fiddling competition, Ottawa Valley style. Ben's right foot tapped to the rhythm and it was her turn to tease him. She threatened to give him fiddling classes for Christmas, and then it occurred to her that the gift might not end up being a joke, that maybe Ben would really like to learn to fiddle, and that, too, made her smile. When the stage switched to the children's talent show, Ben led Maxine out of the tent and through the alleyways of the carnival grounds, past a stilt-walker and a juggler, past giant panda bears hanging tantalizingly as backdrops to the games of chance, past tired mothers pushing strollers, past crying children reaching their hands upward for bright balloons that drifted away from them toward the clouds.
Ben stopped at the midway.
"I can't," Maxine said.

Ben was the one who liked the adrenaline rush of rapids and roller coasters, not her. Then she saw his disappointment and changed her mind; she could do this.

"But only one ride," she said. "That's it."

The carnie impatiently motioned for Maxine to step into the rollercoaster. He snapped the bar in place that held them in, and waved at the next cluster of people to board. Maxine thought about the billy goat and fleeing, but the rollercoaster had begun to move, and there was nothing she could do but ride it. Her heart beat in her throat like the frantic fluttering of a bird caught in a net. The rollercoaster started its slow upward climb, the eye of calm at the centre of the storm, and then they were at the peak of the track, the brief stoppage that marks a shift in direction. Then the descent, slow at first, her heart still beating in her throat like a fragile frightened bird. The ride gathered speed, and Maxine clutched Ben's arm, pressed her fingertips into his skin. She screamed, and then screamed again, and once more, so that her voice sounded behind her, her terror and excitement trailing her physical body, like the tail of a comet.

When the ride ended, Maxine felt faint. She sat on the ground, right where she was, in the midst of the carnival-goers, sat on the stone path in the centre of a forest of legs. The world spun, as if given a sudden and swift flick, God fiddling with the globe on His office desk, and Maxine held her head as if it might come off in her hands. But then the spinning of the world finally slowed, and stopped altogether.

"I'm sorry," Ben said. "I shouldn't have talked you into taking the ride."

Maxine stood up, brushed the pebbles off the seat of her pants.

"Don't apologize," she said. "That was wonderful, all of it."

Before they left the fair, they stood at the cotton candy booth, watched the whisking of the pink clouds on paper cones as if the simple making of cotton candy was precious. Maxine pressed her palms and nose against the plexi-glass that separated them from the gypsy woman who performed this magic. The fluffing of the floss stirred up wisps of memory, and Maxine stepped back, leaving behind marks on the window, the foggy haze of her breath, the small circular imprint of the end of her nose, the round pads of her fingertips, evidence that she had been there, had *been*.

CHAPTER 28

Is it enough, having had *been*?
    Ironically, in some strange way, Maxine was my ghost as much as I was her ghost. Maxine hadn't left the building, or should I say the cave, residue remaining in some corner of my soul as if food at the bottom of a pot.
    Golda believed that ghosts left imprints. Shimmering mirages. Afterlife fingerprints. I was struck with the absurdity of Maxine hovering ghost-like in my cave. Me and my shadow, but who was the shadow?
    Neither it seemed. It wasn't Maxine, shimmering or otherwise, that appeared in my cave. My angel appeared, hunchbacked like a gargoyle, but nevertheless, chisel-perfect. I laughed aloud, as if his reappearance in my otherworld was the joke that shook the cosmos, that put the ghost-shimmer into the stars.
    "Ironic, isn't it?" he said.
    "That you came back, yet once again?"
    "I go where I'm sent. No irony there. You call this cramped smelly hole-in-the-wall heavenly, but not once did you use that adjective to describe your stay in the real thing, paradise."
    I sniffed at the air. Smelly? Slight scent of bear, but that

was all.

It *is* ironic, I thought, not the smell of bear, or the duality of Maxine and my ghost natures, but my use of the word "heavenly."

"It's all relative," the angel added.

"You've been talking to Albert! How's the old fart?"

The angel bristled. The tips of his wings stood up, like hair on the back of a person's neck. I thought maybe the word fart had offended him, but I was wrong.

"Einstein - the old fart - doesn't have the corner on relativity. Do you want me to deliver my message or not?"

I hadn't realized there was a message.

Should have, social visits and angels, an oxymoron.

My angel pulled himself up until he was magnificent. Filled the cave. Wings spread to the full width of their glory. A light emanated from his body. I swear he glowed. It gave his exterior an oiled effect, a heightened polished-marble look, each muscle, each feather, clearly defined. Precision of body. Perfection. Too bad the message didn't live up to the packaging. The message might be the medium, but in the case of my angel, there was a credibility gap between the two.

"The cave is heavenly because of relative time," he announced. "The storm behind you and the promise of the not-yet ahead of you."

"That's it?"

The performance lacked *zing* – content and delivery. He needed to modulate his voice. Add special effects. A bolt of lightning. The sound of trumpets. Props to liven up the spoken word. A cherub or two, the heavenly hosts. No wonder Michael and Gabriel got the good assignments.

"That's it?" I repeated, like an off-stage line prompt girl.

"That's it for now," my angel said.

His shoulders caved forward, as if the delivery of the message had taken some wind out of his sails, or his wings. I remembered his telepathic abilities and regretted my thoughts. "It's a fine message," I said, in case his feelings had been hurt, if that were possible. If angels had feelings, had emotions, or

if these were attributes of humans alone, those who lived and those who had once lived.
The promise of the not-yet.
I sighed with the pleasure of those words.
Not yet.
The words carried reprieve, mid-January in Canada, a thick goose-feather duvet, activities on hold because of a blizzard. No buses running, no schools open, no work places, no roads clear because the snow plow couldn't get through. The promise of the not-yet. That was my message. Not such a bad message after all. I sank into the furs. Sank into the heavenly pleasure of this not-yet. The angel folded his wings into his body in an action more in common with a bat than a bird. He squeezed his large frame out of the small opening of the cave. A tight fit. I watched with interest. Too quickly, he disappeared into the storm. A blast of cold air rushed to fill the vacuum. A jumping bean of panic scrambled inside of me. I had no idea the length of a not-yet. I poked my head out of the cave. The bite of the cold air made me feel alive and I liked the feeling. I thought it was night, but that was only intuition, perhaps simply a result of hibernation, everything seeming like night. The storm raged on with no hint of dying, the swirling of snow blotting out the time of day.
"When will you be back?" I yelled into the fury.
An answer returned to me on the wings of a wind.
"At the time of the flood."
"What flood?" I shouted.
But this time no words returned, not on the wings of the wind, nor the wings of an angel. He was gone, and I was alone again. I wondered if blood beat through his marble body. Probably not, at least not blood-red blood. Probably silver blood, like mercury. Crystal blood, like water. Blood like water from a pristine mountain spring. Water so cold it is almost ice, the precise moment of the not-yet.
Albert didn't like being wrong, at least being told such. He stayed away from my head, oh I don't know, let's say for the sake of relating the story, an eon or so, maybe longer. "How could I have missed it?" he chuckled when he finally returned,

chuckling in that distinct Einstein-ish manner, forgetting (or choosing to forget) our previous disagreement. Albert steered clear of the topic of gambling and dice. Stuck to safer ground. "It affects everything. The whole equation. An oversight of monumental significance, on my part," he said. "It's quite ironic, really."

"What's ironic? The cave as heavenly," I asked, "or the length of my lifeline, winding across my palm and around my wrist like the serpent in the Garden of Eden, compared to Adeline's non-existent lifeline, my sister who, by the way, is still very much alive? Or that I write an obituary and then I get bonked at the side of the road with a tire iron? Or the fact that when I finally decided to become a mother, to have the baby, I miscarried and the baby died?"

"Much too specific," Einstein replied. "The point of the matter is irony itself. Irony's the constant. It permeates everything."

"Oh," I said, as if I should have realized.

$E = MC^2 + irony$.

✧ ✧ ✧

Maxine finished the research for her article about the medical isotopes, inputting her handwritten notes from an interview into her laptop, storing them on her hard drive and her jump drive as an extra precaution, printing up as well a hard copy. She had another interview planned for the next morning, but it had been cancelled, and so she decided to cut her trip short and return to Deep River early. It would be good to see Ben, surprise him. He wouldn't be expecting her. She felt pleased by the unexpected luck of a cancelled interview.

Along the highway north, at a spur of the moment, Maxine pulled the car to the shoulder, stopped at a roadside booth to buy an apple. Another spur of the moment action, she didn't immediately return to the car, but climbed to the top of a large granite rock. There she stood, surveying her surroundings, the Ottawa River, the dark strip of blue-grey mountains at the other side, the largeness of the sky.

Maxine slipped off her sandals. The rock was hard, held warmth, hoarded the sun. She loved the strength, the feel of granite against her feet. She sat down, stretched out her legs, bit into the Macintosh. It was hard and red, the way an apple was supposed to be, crisped by the night frost. She shivered at the taste. Home, it seemed, was not always a house, or a family, or friends. It could be a bite into a crisp apple, the hardness of granite beneath bare feet.

Maxine lay back on the rock, stretched out fully.

The sun shone above her in that way that is autumn in Ontario, bright and without regret, without hesitancy, certain of itself and its place in the unfolding of the seasons, certain of its role in the unfolding of this season. She wriggled out of her worn jacket kept in the car for just such times, rolled it into a log, and put it under her head, watched the sky move above her. And then she slept.

The sweet blessings of the not-yet.

When Maxine woke, she vaguely remembered dreaming, tugged at the string of the dream to unravel it, Ben and her sitting on the front steps of their small house, deep in conversation, but try as she might she couldn't remember what they had been saying. The sun had shifted position in the sky, starting its downward journey, and Maxine felt chilled. She sat up, unwrapped the jacket, shook it. Something fell out of the pocket, caught a glint of the setting sun, rested against the granite. Maxine reached down, picked up the thin silver chain, held it between her fingers so that the charm twirled, Buddha spinning cross-legged in lotus position.

She had forgotten about the necklace.

When had she shoved it into her jacket?

How long had it been sitting there, waiting for this particular moment?

Maxine moved her hands upward to put the chain around her neck, and then stopped. She didn't need the charm anymore, didn't need to declare herself to others. Didn't need a shield or a protective omen, a cross to the vampire. Maxine lowered the chain into her palm, closed her hand around the charm. She thought about throwing the Buddha into the air, the charm flying from the table-rock of granite and through the blue autumn sky, soaring through the air while twirling around itself, somersaulting through space, chain dangling behind like the tail of a kite. And then she did.

Maxine took one last look around her, breathed deeply, sucked the day into her lungs, the flaming leaves, the hard pink-brown granite, the river, the mountains, the sun, the large sky. Then she tugged on her jacket and sandals, climbed back down the large granite rock, trekked the path to her car for the journey home.

After about two hours of driving, Maxine slammed her foot on the brake. Her body lurched forward and she heard the screech of her tires. The animal that she had risked her life to save, the raccoon, stood bathed by the headlights. Its eyes were large, the black circles like ghoul makeup so that the pupils appeared even larger, protection from predators, to deceive carnivores into thinking they were eyeballed in the dark by a bear or a wolf or a monster of unknown origin. Butterflies did the same, years of evolution, natural selection, the favouring of genes, until large black circles the size and appearance of bird's eyes marked the center of their wings.

The highway was dark and silent and wooded. Maxine dimmed her lights to break the spell on the raccoon. It scurried off, disappearing into the gully, reappearing on the other side as a dark shadow, then getting lost in the night and the bush. Maxine turned her lights back on, checked the time on the dashboard. If all went according to plan, she would be home within the hour. She shifted her foot from the brake to the gas pedal, no butterfly wings or raccoon eyes to protect her from predators. No street lamps marked the journey, only the unbroken yellow line that led to the future like Dorothy's yellow brick road. The night was thick at this portion of the highway. Even the trees were thick, as if they hid mysteries, not gentle mysteries, but those that frightened with the stark cruelty of fairytales. Witches with appetites for flesh, woodsmen who carve out hearts dripping with blood, strange ugly creatures that steal little children away into the night, and dying princesses.

Maxine pushed the gas pedal only as much as she dared, wanting to balance the desire to be home with safety, afraid she would miss a curve and end up in a ditch, or the bog, or smash into a tree. Fog rose quickly from the marsh at the side of the road, and then just as quickly dissipated, until the next curve, when it would rise again. She hadn't passed another car for miles now and flicked on her bright beams. Even then she didn't notice the car on the shoulder, not at first, so intent she was on navigating the twists and turns of the highway. She drew up parallel before she saw it, turned to catch the front hood lifted up as she passed by, the outline stark and almost surreal against the backdrop of the trees. She thought about what to do, wanted to get home to see Ben, to crawl into bed with him, to fall asleep. It occurred to her that it wasn't safe to stop. She looked into the rearview mirror, saw the dark shape at the side of the car. Couldn't tell if it were a man or woman, didn't know if there were a child asleep in a car seat, if someone were hurt, pushed the fear of her own safety away, made a decision. All these thoughts, passing through her mind in a split second, the speed of thought a relative thing, like all else, each thing existing in correlation to another, having relevance only in terms of the other. Maxine pulled her car to the shoulder, put the car into park, left it idling, stepped out into the night and began the short walk back, in reality, the longest walk of her short life, all things being relative.

CHAPTER 20

Maxine once asked Ben long ago - before the pregnancy, before the miscarriage, before he left her, before he returned, before so much - if he thought an elephant could die of grief, as a newspaper article she was reading claimed.

"Do you believe everything in the newspaper?" Ben answered.

"Of course not," Maxine lied. "Journalists know better."

Maxine examined the accompanying photo. A lot of living had gone into that elephant. The elephant was old and its skin hung in grey flabs about its skeleton, loose around the ankles like knee socks that wouldn't stay up. According to the story, the elephant had struck up a friendship with a lamb at the zoo. They were inseparable. When the lamb died, the elephant couldn't be consoled. It refused to eat, refused to drink, refused to respond to the games with which the zoo staff tried to distract it, the showering water baths, the delicacies, the delightful foods, the companionship, other animals, other elephants, but to no avail. The elephant would have none of it.

"Yes, an elephant could die of grief," a voice said.

Maybe it was Buddha, maybe Einstein, maybe my angel.

Maybe even The Voice, although I am sure it was my angel who added, "The flood," and I began to sob.

Tears gathered in a pool on the cave floor. Tears expanded to fill my container, lapped against the rock walls. Tears gushed out the cave opening, liquid seeking its own level. Salt stung my eyes, and my sobbing turned into wailing, grew louder, as if the urgent sound of sirens, emergency vehicles in the night, death and life, life and death.

The current of tears swept me along so that my shoulder banged against stone, and then I was outside the cave, where the current tossed me to the surface. Waves batted me into the air and then reclaimed me, and still I wailed, riding the whitewater of this raging river, riding my outrage. Even so, I did not fight the current, swim in the opposite direction, look for shore or a rock or a log upon which to climb, an overhanging branch to grab, a lifeline or a rescue boat, such was my sorrow. I gave myself up completely to the river. Finally, the river gave up too and the salt of my tears buoyed me at the surface, kept me there. I spread my arms and legs wide like a star, floated on my grief. Night and stars stretched above me as far as I could see. The stars shimmered like fireflies, then gathered strength, sizzling like sparklers that children hold in the dark at fireworks, sticks with stars at the end, spitting sparks into the night, a million children holding a million sparklers, a million magic wands. I closed my eyes, and even with my eyes closed, I still saw the stars. The stars were inside my head, universes within my head. I slipped into the darkness, Maxine's universe held safely inside of me.

Ben and Maxine sat on the front step of the porch of their small war-four house in Deep River. Summer bloomed all around them. So much life. The garden edging the front of the house and the driveway tumbled with wild growth, bluebells and morning glories and hollyhocks and daisies and daylilies and columbines and ferns and roses and phlox and zinnias and bachelor buttons and flowering pea plants, all spilling into each other and over the walkways and lawn. Butterflies flitted about the garden and bees sank deeply into the petals. The air was hot and thick and humid. Maxine felt the oxygen against her skin and she breathed deeply, drinking the atmosphere into herself.

"There's a slight change in the air," Ben said. "Do you notice it?"

She did. Fall was in the air. At the edge of a dream like a ruffle on a curtain.

The birds noticed the change, too. Maxine could tell in the watching. They had put aside the frenzy of mating, the frantic busy-ness of nest building and raising their young, the idyllic branch-sitting and singing of empty nests, put all this aside. They held prolonged flight in their wings, in their bodies, soaring longer before settling to roost, stretching their wings, beating them madly to strengthen their muscles, gathering in gaggles and murders and flocks and bevies, preparing themselves for migration.

"How do the birds know their way south in the fall and then back again in the spring?" Maxine asked.

It seemed impossible, really.

"They see their way," Ben said. "Literally. They see Earth's electromagnetic field where we see nothing. It's like a beacon. They align themselves to the beacon. Newts, too. And fish, and butterflies."

"Do people?" Maxine asked. "Can they see their way back?"

A million stars spread out before me in my dream, a million solar systems. Planets spinning around like whirling dervishes, like spinning Buddhas. It was enough to make Maxine's head spin. My head spun, the dream slipstreaming into first person, a smooth transition, no difference really between Maxine and me. I am, she is. I was, she was. Present tense, past tense.

One star caught my attention.

The star pulsated differently, although that wasn't the all of it. It had a strange hue, a tinge that set it apart, like Mars is set apart in the night sky when seen from Earth. But this star was blue, a dazzling electric blue, a blue like nothing I had ever witnessed before, whether dead or alive or some state in-between. I turned and aligned myself with the star. The blue star grew in magnitude and intensity until I was bathed in its light, and I realized that the star had not moved, but it was me that travelled. I felt the blazing rush of speed against my body. I raced through space like a meteor, or a ray of light or faster than light, I don't know. Raced toward what, I don't know. Heard the sound of time pressing against my ears, life whooshing out of me, whooshing me down the tunnel of my own death, or was it the wail of sirens gaining strength in the distance, police and ambulance rushing to rescue me at the side of the dark road, to pull me from the edge, the message from my angel, not-yet.

I have hope.
Always hope.

ACKNOWLEDGEMENTS

First and always, thank you to my immediate circle of family, Bob and Samantha Paul. You are my cosmos - the sun and planets around which this whirling dervish turns. Thank you as well to my parents, Marjorie and Arthur Lane. May they enjoy their paradise - whatever or wherever that may be. Also my deep thanks to Veronica Ross and Elaine Auerbach for their close attention to detail when reading the manuscript and providing editing comments. Thank you to my good friend, Leslie Bamford, for always being there. Thank you to the Dove Tale community of writers for patiently working through the many incarnations (and many years) of this story - Netty Meyer, Robert Bamford, Leslie Bamford, Veronica Ross, Dianne Whitman, Shirley Hartung, Matthew Bin, John Boulden, Bob Paul, Christine White Woods and Gary Kreller. And finally, thank you to the person who has made the publication of my third novel a reality, Robert Morgan - I am grateful for his vision, dedication, and determination to make BookLand Press and its writers an enduring part of the Canadian literary landscape.

ALSO BY MARIANNE PAUL

Tending Memory

PUBLISHER: BookLand Press

ISBN: 978-09780838-5-4

GENRE: Fiction

FORMAT: Trade Paperback

SIZE: 8.5" x 5.5"

PRICE: $25.95

PUBLICATION: June 2007

Abandoned at an early age, one parent simply packing and leaving, the other suffering an unexpected death, Michaela is raised by her grandparents. Precocious and independent, she runs away for the first time when she is four, and for the final time when she is fifteen. To survive on the street, Michaela scams her way to food and a dry place to sleep. She meets Thomas when she hides out in a seminary library, disguising her female body in baggy clothes, passing time reading books on the lives of the church fathers and saints. A scholar and would-be priest, Thomas thinks he is simply doing a good deed when he invites the runaway to stay with him.

Michaela doesn't look like the gypsy traveller she claims to be. Pale as the moon, body rake-thin, hair cropped short and the colour of corn silk, she weaves with gypsy ardor the tale of her Rom origin and her olive-skinned parents. With each new telling, the currents of story and memory shift like the direction of the wind along the open road.

To Michaela, home is not a location. She carries it with her in the same way she carries her memories. She is always destined to leave.

ALSO BY MARIANNE PAUL

Twice in a Blue Moon

PUBLISHER: BookLand Press

ISBN: 978-0-9783793-3-9

GENRE: Fiction

FORMAT: Trade Paperback

SIZE: 8.5" x 5.5"

PRICE: $25.95

PUBLICATION: December 2007

When Aley Pierce writes, her words don't stay on the page but spill into reality. Or so her neighbours think, who see her words as evil. Tensions escalate into an organized campaign of book banning and book burning, until Aley herself doubts who she is and what she does.

A century and a half earlier, Elizabeth Barnes' talent for water dowsing unearths a body in her neighbour's field. Under growing accusations that she is a witch, Elizabeth is blamed for the drought that puts a stranglehold on the small farming community.

But water dowsing isn't Elizabeth's only talent – she is a clairvoyant. Does she see the future or create it? Even Elizabeth doesn't know.

Beneath the unfolding of the blue moon, events resurface across time, and the lives of the two women interlink. Does Aley create Elizabeth, or is Elizabeth dreaming Aley?